They were completely and utterly alone.

Meg was conscious of the quick rise and fall of Erik's broad chest as their spat of moments ago morphed into something hotter and more dangerous.

"This is stupid," she said, as much to herself as to him. "I don't like you. I don't trust you. I shouldn't be attracted to you."

"Same goes," he said, a flash of desire crossing his face. "Then again, that seems to be my usual M.O. What's your excuse?"

But even though his words came out fairly mocking, he closed the distance between them until she could feel the warmth of him against the suddenly sensitized skin of her cheeks and lips. "Stupidity, maybe. The circumstances. Hell, even the danger. I don't know."

But she did. That last choice resonated a little too well, but the moment was lost when he closed the gap between them. Their lips touched. Their breaths mingled.

And their last shreds of rationality were lost.

JESSICA ANDERSEN

RED ALERT

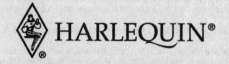

TORONTO • NEW YORK • LONDON
AMSTERDAM • PARIS • SYDNEY • HAMBURG
STOCKHOLM • ATHENS • TOKYO • MILAN • MADRID
PRAGUE • WARSAW • BUDAPEST • AUCKLAND

ISBN-13: 978-0-373-22945-1
ISBN-10:   0-373-22945-3

RED ALERT

ABOUT THE AUTHOR

Though she's tried out professions ranging from cleaning sea lion cages to cloning glaucoma genes, from patent law to training horses, Jessica is happiest when she's combining all these interests with her first love: writing romances. These days she's delighted to be writing full-time on a farm in rural Connecticut that she shares with a small menagerie and a hero named Brian. She hopes you'll visit her at www.JessicaAndersen.com for info on upcoming books, contests and to say hi!

Books by Jessica Andersen

HARLEQUIN INTRIGUE

*Bear Claw Creek Crime Lab

CAST OF CHARACTERS

Megan Corning—Her medical research is poised to revolutionize prenatal genetic testing, but the technique has a darker side. When a series of "accidents" threaten Meg's life, a handsome stranger protects her—but his motives are far from pure.

Erik Falco—Once a cop, now a hugely successful businessman, Erik has vowed to acquire the rights to the cutting-edge research. But how far will he go once he meets the lovely Dr. Corning?

Zachary Cage—The head administrator of Boston General Hospital must weigh the value of the new technology against the needs of the hospital and the safety of his employees.

Raine Montgomery—Erik's second-in-command has something to hide.

Annette Foulke—She wants the tenured university position that Megan seems sure to win.

Luke Cannon—Is it a coincidence that the head of acquisitions at Pentium Pharmaceuticals is a member of Meg's climbing gym?

Edward—The youth hides beneath the hood of a dark sweatshirt and listens to the voices that tell him he has only one chance to make things right.

Prologue

Edward slipped through the front door of the hospital unnoticed. Bodies thronged the main atrium, a lunchtime press of patients and personnel that made it easy for him to cross the lobby unnoticed in his jeans and dark hooded sweatshirt. From there, he walked to the brushed-steel elevators that led to the Reproductive Technology offices. Then he waited.

And watched.

He sneered at the men and women who passed his vantage point, some alone, some in couples, all united by hope. The desire to create a new life. A new beginning.

Garbage, he thought with a quiet snort. There was no such thing as a new beginning. You only got one life, and if you screwed it up, you were out of luck.

Then again, his mother used to say, *You've got to make your own luck. Nobody else is going to make it for you.*

That was what he was doing. Making his own luck.

"Are you sure about this?" a female voice asked nearby.

Edward turned to see a dark-haired woman clinging to the free arm of an even darker-haired man. Though the guy looked to be in his late thirties, he used a gray metal cane to hitch along on a leg that didn't bend quite right.

"It's just a blood test," the guy said, voice sharp, as though he'd answered the question before. He glanced down and his expression softened a degree. "I wouldn't endanger you or the baby."

"Of course," the woman murmured as the elevator doors whooshed open, inviting them in. She didn't sound convinced, nor did she release the gimp's arm as the two of them stepped into the elevator.

The doors hissed shut, leaving Edward staring after the couple. A faint smile touched his lips as he reached up and pulled his sweatshirt hood forward so he could see out but nobody could see in.

Today was going to be his lucky day.

Chapter One

Exhaustion thrummed through Megan Corning's body, a combination of too many grant applications and too few days off in the past months.

Knowing she didn't have time to be tired yet, Meg dug her fingers into her red-gold hair and told herself to focus on something else. Something positive, like the new office the Boston General Hospital administrators had given her just the week before.

She glanced around the room and grimaced.

The walls were painted a classy ice-blue and hung with a handful of diplomas and accolades. The front cover of last March's *Science* magazine was smack in the center, announcing a "New Noninvasive Method for Prenatal Diagnosis." If her desk were a bed, it would've been a California king, and the rolling chair was real leather.

It all looked very impressive. Hell, what she'd done *was* impressive. But the wall art, added to the stark white padded chairs opposite her black metal desk, gave the decor a chilly feeling.

The room was *so* not her.

At least, it wasn't how she saw herself. She had a sneaking suspicion the austere furniture and harsh lighting were perfectly aligned with how too many of her co-workers saw her. Functional. Dependable. Lacking warmth.

And why is that?

She closed her eyes and rubbed her temples, knowing she'd created the image herself a decade earlier, on her father's orders that she tone down her reputation when he got her the job at Boston General.

Well, not orders, precisely. Call it a strong suggestion from Dad. Who also happened to be a Nobel Prize–winning scientist.

Tone down the dangerous stuff, Meg, Robert Corning had said in his resonant lecturer's voice. *They already doubt your science, why give them an excuse to criticize your sense?*

As much as she'd hated to admit it, he'd had a point. Her insistence on proving that a baby's cells could be found in the mother's bloodstream had already raised too many eyebrows. Her grades hadn't been the best, and her Ph.D. thesis had been long on theory, short on results.

Of necessity, she'd grown out the streaks in her hair, put her skis, parachutes and other toys into storage, and focused on figuring out how to test a baby's genetic makeup from a sample of the mother's blood.

They said it couldn't be done, but she'd managed it. She'd developed a blood test that was poised to revolutionize prenatal genetic analysis. Boston General Hospital and her cosponsor, Thrace University, would reap the rewards and Meg would be assured tenure. She'd be set for life—she'd have a job, a good salary, a whopping pension and a corner office.

"And it won't be black and white!" she said out loud.

A head popped around the open office door. "You need me, boss?"

"Um, no. I was talking to myself, actually." Meg grimaced when Jemma Smoltz, her patient coordinator and sometimes lab assistant, stepped into the room.

Short, dark hair framed Jemma's pixie-perfect face, and she wore flirty capri pants that showed off her slim ankles, one of which was tattooed with a pink rose.

She was twenty-six, tiny and feminine, and she made thirty-four-year-old, five-foot-ten Meg feel like a human water buffalo in comparison.

Less so these days, though, because Meg had been working out. She'd lost fifteen pounds since winter, and had her sights set on another ten.

Jemma grinned. "Daydreaming about that stud rock climbing instructor at your new gym?"

Meg rolled her eyes. "I never should have told you about Otto." But there was no harm in it, really. She was just window shopping, admiring the kind of active, muscle-bound hunk she'd always found attractive.

"You should ask him out."

"Not on your life. He's too young for me. And besides—" Meg waved at the diplomas, the glossy magazine cover and the cool blue walls "—that's not my lifestyle anymore. I can't take off on a moment's notice to free climb God only knows where." Though there were sure days she wished she could. "I've got a lab. Responsibilities."

Jemma wrinkled her nose. "That doesn't mean you have to be boring."

"I'm not boring, I'm focused. There's a difference." Although some days, she worried that there wasn't any difference at all. That she wasn't pretending to be boring anymore—she'd actually *become* boring.

Hell, even her recent return to free climbing was on an indoor wall with landing pads on the floor.

Unusually annoyed with her office, with herself, Meg reached across her desk and flipped open the next folder on a stack of twenty, hoping Jemma would get the hint.

"Aw, come on," the younger woman wheedled. "You owe it to yourself to ask Otto—"

"I owe it to the hospital to collect another fifty beta test subjects before the end of the week," Meg snapped. "Is the next patient here?"

Her assistant's answer was a long, slow grin. "You're thinking about it."

"Just shut up and send in the patient, will you?"

But once Jemma was gone, Meg looked around the sterile-seeming room, then down at the edges of clothing visible beneath her lab coat. The green pullover, tan suede skirt and tall brown boots had seemed smart and professional that morning.

Now they're boring, she thought. Maybe Jemma had a point. Maybe it *was* time to do something different, time to—

"Mr. and Mrs. Phillips," Jemma announced from the doorway.

Nope. It was time to get to work.

Meg stood and moved around the ginormous desk as the couple entered the room. "I'm Dr. Corning. Please call me Meg." She focused her attention on Mrs. Phillips first, because it was the woman's body they'd be discussing. Her child. Her blood sample.

The wife was a knockout. She wore expensive-looking navy wool pants and sensibly flat shoes, topped with an Empire-waisted tunic that flowed down past her hips, obscuring any evidence of the early term pregnancy she'd reported in her initial interview with Jemma. Her glossy brunette hair was swept into a soft French braid, and her brown eyes and full, dusky lips were accented with fashionable hints of purpley brown makeup that made her features pop.

But her eyes held a distinct flicker of nerves when she took Meg's hand in a brief clasp. "I'm Raine, and this is my husband, Erik."

The pause before the word *husband* was almost imperceptible, but Meg tucked it in her mental files before she turned and extended her hand. "It's a pleasure to meet you, Erik."

Then she got a good look at him and had her own moment of hesitation.

The guy made a hell of a first impression.

His clothes matched Raine's, not in color, but in the understated taste and quality of the fall-weight, steel-gray suit, dove-gray oxford shirt and gunmetal tie. The monochromatic scheme might have washed another man out, but it complemented this one, emphasizing both his angular face and the faint silver frost that touched the edges of his blue-black hair. He was tall, topping Meg by a good four inches or so, and his shoulders were broad beneath the tapered suit jacket.

His eyes were a deep, nearly sapphire-blue, and they narrowed when he took her hand and held it a beat too long. "The pleasure is mine."

Meg dampened an instant shimmer of attraction—he was another woman's husband, after all. She gestured toward the chairs opposite her desk. "Take a seat and tell me a little bit about yourselves."

Raine sank into one of the chairs, but Erik remained standing. Then, as though realizing that Meg wouldn't sit until he did, he grabbed his chair and pulled it a few inches away from his wife. It wasn't until he braced himself to step forward that Meg realized he carried a gunmetal-gray cane nearly the color of his tie. He leaned on it with the ease of long practice as he lowered himself to the chair, right leg braced stiffly in front of his body.

He stared at her, eyes saying, *Don't you dare pity me,* but out loud, he said, "What do you want to know?"

His wife frowned. "I thought we were here for a

blood test. We already filled out the questionnaire and your assistant took a preliminary sample." She pushed up the bell sleeve of her tunic to show a small Band-Aid at the crook of her elbow. "Isn't this just a formality?"

Meg smiled. "I need to make sure you understand the study structure and your privacy rights." She paused, losing her place in the oft-repeated speech as Erik shifted uncomfortably in the upholstered chair.

He looked up and caught her staring. His eyes glinted with an expression she couldn't interpret and wasn't sure she liked. But he said, "Can you tell us a little bit about the test? My—Raine is a cautious woman."

Another hesitation? Meg thought. Wonder what sort of marriage these two have.

Telling herself it was really none of her business, she pushed a glossy folder across the desk. "Here's some information for you to take home and look over later. Most of it is also on our Web site." She slid a brochure from the folder and tapped a color schematic cutaway of a pregnant woman. "We're in the final stages of streamlining prenatal blood tests for a number of common genetic disorders. The technique is called Noninvasive Prenatal Testing, NPT for short. We're enrolling pregnant women in their first or second trimester, and asking that you come in for biweekly blood draws." Meg smiled at Raine's indrawn breath. "It's just one milliliter at a time, so we won't drain you dry. We're not vampires."

"Twice a week is a substantial time commitment

for me." Raine glanced at her husband, whose attention was focused elsewhere. She touched his knee. "Erik, don't you think twice a week is too much for me to be out of the office?"

He diverted his gaze from the wall art and glanced at her. "I'm sure your boss will give you the time." His lips twitched. "He's not all that bad, you know."

The two traded a look that excluded Meg. The sense of connection sent a slice of harmless envy through her chest.

Maybe Jemma was right. Maybe she *had* been neglecting her social life for too long. Maybe it was time to meet a man, someone she could hike and bike and climb with, someone who loved all the things she used to love.

As soon as the licensing went through and tenure was announced, she promised herself. Then she'd focus on moving from ice-blue walls to something more interesting.

Maybe teal. Hot pink.

Sapphire blue.

Focus, Meg! She gave herself a mental shake and continued her explanation. "We're testing whether the different phases of pregnancy affect our results. In addition, we'll be able to examine your baby for most known genetic diseases. We can—"

"Some people say that's impossible," Erik interrupted. His attention wasn't on the wall art anymore. Now it was focused on Meg. "Plenty of experts in the field say your results are nothing but false positives and hopeful interpretation."

Normally, Meg would have taken the challenge and explained the strength of her science. But now she paused as her instincts jangled a warning.

Something told her that this guy wasn't quite what he seemed.

She forced a smile. "I see you've done your homework, Mr. Phillips."

"Call me Erik." He leaned forward, hitching his weight to the left to ease his bad leg. "And yes, I've done some background reading. Three of the top experts in the field of prenatal testing have publicly denounced your discovery."

"Only because I beat them to it."

"They say it's impossible to isolate a baby's cells from maternal blood."

"Not impossible," Meg countered. "Even dinosaurs like Lafitte in Paris and Heinz Kramer in Dusseldorf admit that fetal cells and DNA are carried in the maternal bloodstream for years, sometimes even decades after the pregnancy. They simply don't believe that it's possible to isolate the one-in-a-million fetal cell and use it for testing."

"And you believe it's possible?"

"I've done it," she said simply, and with a bone-deep sense of pride for the work that would help so many. No more pregnancies would be lost due to a misdirected amniocentesis needle or a nick during chorionic villus sampling, two of the most common—and invasive—procedures used for prenatal genetic testing.

"How does it work?" he asked, eyes revealing nothing.

She tapped the brochure. "The process is summarized here."

He dismissed the schematic with a wave. "I've read what's posted on the Web site, but how does it really work? How exactly do you isolate the fetal cells? Is it true that the baby's cells can sometimes heal the mother if she's injured?"

"That hasn't been proven to my satisfaction," Meg said, a chill chasing through her bloodstream, because she had no intention of pursuing the question. Not now. Not ever. Not with the risks involved. "I'm sorry, but I'm not at liberty to discuss the specifics of the process."

Especially not until next month, when the last of the patents would finally be filed.

A handful of university glitches had delayed the applications, leaving her in a legal gray area. If another researcher—or worse, one of the big drug companies—tried to scoop her work, she was in trouble. Though she had her lab notes, patent battles were notoriously long and messy, and neither Boston General nor Thrace University could stand up to one of the big companies if it came down to lawyers and money.

Be careful, her father had cautioned when he'd been in town the week before. *Your work is at its most vulnerable right now. They know you've done it, but not how, and they'll be itching for that one detail, the one trick that lets you do what everyone said couldn't be done.*

With that caution ringing in her ears, Meg narrowed her eyes. "Why do you ask?"

"No reason, really." Raine touched her husband's arm, urging him to relax. "Ever since I found out about the pregnancy, Erik's been fascinated by the technology."

He shot her an unreadable look, but shrugged with a half smile that did little to lighten the intensity of his face. "Sorry. Occupational hazard."

"You're an engineer?" Meg asked. She glanced quickly at Raine's questionnaire.

"No, I'm—" A muted buzz cut him off midsentence. He frowned, reached into his coat pocket and pulled out a seriously high-tech communications device—a little handheld that combined a phone, computer, fax and probably a food processor into one unit. He read the display and frowned. "We've got to go."

He didn't show his wife the message and she didn't argue. They rose as one and, despite his bad leg, showed an almost military precision in their actions.

Meg rounded the desk and held the door for them. "Please look over the material and call me if you have any questions. We'll be in touch once the preliminary blood screening is complete." Though she already knew what it would show. "If the blood work looks good, you can decide whether you're willing to make the necessary time commitment in return for free genetic screening for the baby and a small stipend."

She ushered them out and closed the door behind them, knowing damn well she wouldn't see either of them again.

Moments later there was a brisk knock on the door. Jemma opened the panel without waiting for an invite, and raised her eyebrows when she saw that Meg was alone. "Where did Mrs. Phillips go?"

"Let me guess. She's not pregnant." Meg scowled toward the elevators. "It was a setup. A fishing expedition. Who were they working for? TRL? Genticor?"

Jemma shook her head, eyes worried. "I don't know about that, but she's definitely pregnant, and there's a problem. You've got to get her back here, right now."

"You've already got results back on the baby?" Meg asked, confused. Impossible. Her technique was fast, but not *that* fast.

"No, we haven't even started separating out the cells. But Max needed an unknown sample for one of his test runs, so I gave him a small subsample of Raine Phillips's blood."

Max Vasek was Meg's second in command. With two degrees and a decade in research, he could easily have his own lab, but preferred the freedom of working for Meg. He kept the lab running smoothly and followed his own investigative directions on the side. These days, he was working on a panel of accelerated genetic tests for expecting mothers. So new he hadn't yet reported it to the hospital or the university, Max's technique could identify the presence of twenty-plus genetic abnormalities that could endanger the life of mother or child—all in the space of less than fifteen minutes.

A sick pit opened up in Meg's stomach. "Max's technique hasn't been fully validated, and I'm not ready to go public. If we know something, I can't tell them how or why we know it."

He shouldn't have performed the test on an unenrolled patient's DNA. Though they had signed consent for Raine's preliminary sample, the initial forms didn't include blanket consent for all tests. They'd stumbled over into an ethical gray area.

Damn it, Max.

Jemma handed her the printout. "I don't care how you do it, but get her back here. She's heterozygous for both the Factor V Leiden and prothrombin 20210 mutations."

"Oh, hell." Meg was out the door in an instant, headed for the elevators. Halfway there, she called, "Phone down to the front desk and see if they can grab her. She needs to be on supportive therapy, pronto!"

The mutations were ticking time bombs. Separately, they increased the risk of blood clot disorders including strokes, heart attacks and pulmonary embolisms during pregnancy.

Together, they virtually guaranteed a problem. Perhaps even a fatal one.

Suspicions tabled for now, Meg hurried out of the elevator the moment the doors whooshed open on the ground floor. When the security guard shook his grizzled head, she jogged across the lobby and pushed through the revolving doors out onto Kneeland Street.

Boston General perched at the intersection between the swanky theater district and the more eclectic environs of Chinatown. The busy street dividing the two teemed with vehicles and pedestrians, making Meg fear that she might have lost the couple.

Worry flowed through her. If they'd been sent by one of the big companies, they'd probably given false names and contact information. She might be unable to find them, unable to warn Raine that—

There! The pedestrian flow ebbed for a moment and Meg saw a man leaning on a cane as he walked a woman to a taxi.

"Erik!" Meg called. A cement truck—part of the endless construction of Boston General's new wing—revved its engine nearby, drowning out her next shout.

She gritted her teeth and dodged into the sea of bodies on the sidewalk. Some of the pedestrians gave way at the sight of her white coat. Others glared and jostled her as she fought her way to the street.

"Erik, Raine, wait!"

But he didn't climb into the cab with the pregnant woman. Instead he handed her in, shut the door and awkwardly stepped back onto the edge of the sidewalk near the construction zone. Nearby, construction workers directed a heavy stream of cement into a deeply excavated foundation form.

She lunged across the last few feet separating them and grabbed his sleeve. "Erik!"

He turned and his face blanked with surprise. "Dr. Corning. What are you—"

Someone pushed her from behind and she tumbled against him. She felt hard muscle through the elegant suit, then another blow slammed into her, knocking her aside.

She shrieked and stumbled back, arms windmilling. Her hip banged into a railing and wood splintered. The heel of one of her tall boots snagged on something.

She screamed. Overbalanced.

And plunged into the construction pit.

The fall was short, but when she hit, the impact drove the breath from her lungs. Her landing pad was cold and wet. Too heavy to be water, too gritty to be mud.

She'd fallen into the cement form.

And she was sinking.

Over the growing hubbub of screams and shouts from above, she heard a man's voice shout, *"Meg!"*

She looked up and saw Erik leaning over the lip of the cement form. He stretched his arm down and sunlight glinted off his cane. "Grab on!"

Gasping and choking as the wet, heavy weight pressed on every fiber of her being, she reached up. She could just touch the cane with the edge of her fingertips. She stretched farther and heard a rushing roar, and a man's shout.

Above her, the cement truck sluiceway opened up and dumped heavy, clinging cement on top of her.

"Help me!" she screamed. The cascade of wet cement filled the space quickly, covering her shoulders in seconds, then working its way up her neck.

Why hadn't they turned off the sluice? Couldn't the cement truck operator tell there was a problem?

Even as the thought formed in Meg's brain, it was too late. The liquefied silt poured down around her, covering her neck and ears. She screamed, though she knew it would do no good.

She was being buried alive.

Safety was no more than ten feet away. Rescue had to be on its way. But it would be too late.

She screamed again and arched her back against the sluggish give of the setting cement. She looked up to the edge of the cement form, toward the sidewalk, where the protective railing hung askew. Though she could hear nothing over the splatter of cement that continued to fall from above and her eyes were blurred with clinging clumps of grit, she saw the silhouette of a broad-shouldered man in an expensive suit.

The image of blue eyes stayed with her when she sucked in her last breath.

Chapter Two

"Get that crane down here! And kill the flow, *now!*" Erik's ears rang from the equipment noise and the force of his own shouts. "What is wrong with you people? *There's a woman in there!*"

He gripped the edge of the cement form so hard his fingers ached. He cursed the construction crew for being incompetent, and cursed himself for being worse than useless. Eight years ago, he could have jumped in and saved her.

If he jumped in now, there would be two of them stuck, drowning.

The flowing cement cut out with a rattle. The last few blobs plopped into the foundation form and were immediately absorbed by the smooth gray surface.

There was no sign of Meg Corning. No sign of movement.

Panic spiked through Erik. "Damn it! Where's that crane?"

"Here!" a man's voice shouted, and a weighted

ball with a large, dangling hook swung down into the foundation pit.

Erik was aware of the shouting, gesturing pedestrians cramming close to the disaster site, aware of the rising throb of sirens in the near distance. The local cops would be here any moment, but the trapped woman couldn't wait that long.

The thought brought an image of her, a flash of red-gold curls and intelligent hazel eyes, a stacked body hidden beneath a starched white lab coat.

He'd gone to the meeting in person because he'd needed to put a face to the reams of reports he'd amassed on Meg Corning. He'd told himself it was groundwork, but it had been more than that.

It had been a compulsion. He'd needed to see her.

Now he might be the last person to ever see her.

The crane operator finally swung the line toward Erik, who caught the cable. Cursing, he pulled himself onto the swinging weight, braced his good foot on the hook and let the other leg dangle free. Damn thing wasn't good for much else.

"Lower me into the pit," he shouted, waving at the crane operator. "Stop when I give the signal!"

He hung on tight as the crane operator swung him out over the slick gray surface and lowered him toward the cement. Please let it still be liquid, he thought. Please let her be holding her breath.

But that seemed a thin hope. The average person would be struggling. Thrashing. Fighting to get free, only to drive themselves deeper into the muck. The very stillness of the slurry was a problem. Either

Meg Corning had professional-level survival skills or she'd lost consciousness.

Having met the pretty lady doctor, he feared the latter. She didn't seem like the survivalist type.

"Okay, stop!" He waved when the hook was barely skimming the surface of the cement, not wanting to drop the heavy weight on top of her. Then he took two quick breaths, aimed off to the side of the form, away from where she'd fallen—

And jumped.

The impact was like slamming into a solid floor that became liquid the moment he passed through. His bad leg folded, sending agony up his hip. He ignored the pain and fought through the clinging gray grit, which had started to set.

It wouldn't be fully solidified for hours, maybe days, but the partially thickened soup blocked his efforts. She couldn't be more than three feet away, but he couldn't get to her.

Heart pounding, fearing it was already too late, he reached up and grabbed on to the hook, then waved to the operator. "Pull me toward the other side. Slowly!"

Gravel and grit dug into his hands as the hook moved, dragging him through the resisting cement, sparking tortured howls in his bum leg.

Not for the first time, he wished they had just cut the damn thing off.

Then he felt something beneath him. A change in the texture, a hint of cloth and something solid.

"Hold it!" he shouted. "Stop! I've got her."

He looped one arm over the hook and reached down with the other. He felt for a handful of cloth, an arm, something he could use to drag her to the surface.

A strong hand clasped his wrist.

"She's conscious!" he shouted. "Pull me up, quick! No," he contradicted himself, "Slowly. Very slowly."

He didn't want to lose his grip. More importantly, he didn't want to hurt her. The hold of the cement was stronger than he'd expected.

He reached down and grabbed her upper arm, near where it joined her body. As though they'd discussed the plan, she wrapped her arms around his legs and hung on tight.

This time he welcomed the burn of pain that shot up his right hip.

"Okay, pull!"

The crane engine revved above him and the weighted hook lifted. Erik's shoulder joint popped.

The hook rose, but he didn't. A human anchor weighted him down. She was stuck fast, and the seconds counting down in his head told him she didn't have much time left.

Indeed, he felt her grip slacken, sliding in the grit and the grime.

Then her hands fell away. Her body went limp against him and the image of her peaches-and-cream complexion went gray in his mind's eye.

No!

The hook continued to lift. Erik's shoulder and arm burned, but there was no give from below.

He needed more lift, more strength, more leverage. The man he'd been before would have had the tools and the skills, but the man he was now had nothing but a mangled leg.

With a roar of anger at things he couldn't change no matter how much he wanted to, he let go of the trapped, unconscious woman and reached up to grab the ascending hook with both hands. He dragged his legs forward and wrapped them around her body. He locked his good ankle around his bad calf and hung on tight.

If the pins and screws that ached in the dark of winter nights had ever served a purpose, now was the time.

"Lift hard!" he shouted to the operator, and tensed every muscle in his body. The moment the engine surged, he scissored his legs forward, curling his body up in an effort to break the cement hold on her body.

Nothing.

As the clock ticked down past "too late" in his head, he tried again, summoning all of the strength he'd retained, and maybe some remembered from back when he was whole. He pulled himself up toward the hook with his arms and dragged the woman with him, legs vised around her torso.

He felt a shift. A give. And then he was moving upward, toward street level, toward safety.

And he brought Meg Corning along with him.

He heard cheers from the crowd, whoops of sirens and the shouts of local cops creating order. The crane operator lifted him above the crowd, then back down, lowering Erik and his limp burden onto a hastily cleared section of pavement near the broken barrier.

Uniformed officers reached up to take the unconscious woman, who was immediately swarmed by emergency personnel. They left Erik to jump down on his own.

He did, then staggered and nearly fell.

"I've got you." An overweight, balding stranger grabbed him by his sodden suit jacket, righted him, and shoved his cane into his hand. "Here. You'll need this."

Erik stared at the cane, at the ring of polished wood near the handle that made it stronger and weaker at the same time. "You can say that again. Thanks for hanging on to it for me."

"No sweat. I owe you one."

Erik glanced up. "Do I know you?"

"It's not a big deal if you don't remember me, Mr. Falco." The stranger grinned. "You bought out my father's company a couple of years ago. Celltronics. Gave him enough money to retire to a big-assed boat in the Caribbean, and put all the grandkids through college."

"Glad it worked out," Erik said automatically, though he barely remembered the deal, which had been one of too many acquisitions, all aimed at an impossible goal.

Or maybe not so impossible anymore. Not once he got his hands on the NPT technology.

At the thought of the technology and its creator,

he turned toward the knot of rescue personnel nearby. To his surprise, he saw that Meg was conscious, sitting up without assistance while chunks of half-set cement dribbled from her lab coat and dark hair.

And she was glaring daggers at him.

DAMN IT, Meg thought. The bastard had lied to her. And then he'd rescued her.

How was she supposed to react to that?

The aftershocks raced through her body, remnants of those long seconds that she'd been submerged in the cement. She'd told herself to be calm, to remember her old training. *Count your heartbeats,* her skydiving instructor had told her. *It'll keep the panic away.*

And it had. Mostly.

Then Erik Phillips had come for her.

Only he wasn't Erik Phillips. He was Erik Falco, head of FalcoTechno, which was one of the largest technology conglomerates on the eastern seaboard.

And one of the highest bidders trying to buy her upcoming patents.

Piercing blue eyes fixed on her, Falco crossed to where she sat on the bumper of an ambulance, huddled beneath a scratchy wool blanket. "How do you feel?"

"Alive, thanks to you." She tightened the blanket around her shoulders. "I'm not sure why you made the effort, though. It'd be much easier for you to push the deal through with me out of the picture."

He nodded, acknowledging his identity, as well as the standoff that had been handled through lawyers and the hospital administration up to that point. But his expression darkened as he said, "You think I'd let you drown to get the deal done?"

She shrugged, feeling the rasp of drying grit against her skin. "In my experience, the human element doesn't matter much to commercial drug developers."

"Oh. You're one of *them*." He rolled his eyes. "You're one of those researchers who think academia is the only pure science. God forbid someone make a profit off research."

She sniffed. "Let's just say I've had better luck with the university types."

"Why? Because your mother left you and your father for a man with a bigger house and a better bankroll?" Falco stopped and cursed. "I apologize. Please forget I said that." He waved to the hovering paramedics. "Let's get you transported to the ER so the docs can check you out."

"I'm fine." She stood stiffly, feeling her suede skirt and pretty green pullover crackle with the motion. "And no, I won't forget what you said. Don't think you know me because your people did a few background checks. And don't think you can order me around because you saved my life, or because you think that little charade with—" She broke off. "Oh, hell. You've got to get Raine—if that's even her name—back here."

"Why? What's wrong?"

Cautious of patient privacy, Meg said, "Not here. Have your wife—" She saw the shift in his expression and pressed her lips together. "Another lie. Who is she?"

He didn't even have the grace to look ashamed. "Raine Montgomery, vice president of my pharmaceuticals division."

"Lucky for you there was a pregnant woman handy. And lucky for her, too. Have her meet me in the lab in ten minutes."

He scowled. "You won't be in the lab in ten minutes. You'll be in the ER."

Temper fraying with the need to get somewhere alone, somewhere private where she could shake, scream, fall apart, all the things she couldn't do across the street from her office and in full view of countless hospital employees, Meg snapped, "Don't tell me what to do. In fact, leave me the hell alone. I want to see Raine ASAP, but I don't want to see you. Not ever again."

His expression shifted to neutral. "That could be difficult."

She sneered at him. "The way I've heard it, you thrive on a challenge, Mr. Falco. Consider this one."

She turned and pushed through the crowd to the hospital, ignoring the TV reporters' microphones and shouted questions. She left the cops enough information to find her later, after she'd cleaned up. After she'd broken down.

It wasn't until she was halfway across Kneeland Street that she realized her feet were burning. She looked down and stared stupidly at her gray-smeared toes, which were barely covered by torn panty hose.

She'd lost her tall brown boots. They'd been sucked off by the cement, left behind when Erik Falco had risked his own life to drag her out of the muck.

That small detail brought home the danger before she was ready for it. Her stomach knotted on a surge of nausea and her throat closed down until only a trickle of oxygen seeped through.

She was suffocating.

The gray waves closed in on her, surrounding her, compressing her. Killing her.

Not here, Meg told herself. Not now. Not yet. Not where she would cause a scene on hospital property. Her father was right. Her science was controversial enough without her personal exploits adding fuel to the flame. The thought of her dependable, rock-steady sire helped hold off the shakes and she forced her trembling legs to carry her the rest of the way across the street, barefoot.

She thought she heard her name called in deep, masculine tones, but she didn't turn back. If it was one of the officers, he could phone the lab. If it was Falco, he could go to hell.

She had no intention of prostituting her work to some megacompany that cared only for profit.

And if he tried to force the issue with her bosses, she'd fight him tooth and nail.

"DAMN STUBBORN WOMAN." Erik cursed under his breath as she disappeared through the main hospital doors. Then again, why did that surprise him? She'd already managed to block his representatives at every turn, fighting to keep her discovery in the public arena by administering it through the university rather than a private company.

He respected the effort. Too bad it was doomed, because he had no intention of failing. Her fetal cell isolation process would be his, with or without her cooperation. His whole pharma staff was on it.

At the thought of his staff, he grabbed for his cell phone and speed dialed the office. "Get me Raine." When she answered the transfer, he said, "Sorry for the quick turnaround, but I need you back at the hospital right now."

"Another stint as Mrs. Phillips?" Raine asked, her voice carrying an unfamiliar lilt that put him on edge.

Six years earlier, her résumé had overridden his reluctance to work with a pretty, single woman his age, and he'd hired her into the then-startup Falco-Techno. They had grown together, Raine and the company, and she'd proven herself to be an exception to his rules. She was a beautiful woman who kept her mind strictly on business. One he could trust to get his back.

They'd stayed out of each other's personal lives. Hell, he hadn't even realized she'd been married until six weeks earlier, when he'd found her in the men's bathroom, crying, disoriented and puking.

She'd confessed to being pregnant with her husband's baby…a year after the divorce was final.

The experience had forged an uncomfortable

intimacy between Erik and Raine, one he'd tried like hell to ignore until he got word that Dr. Meg Corning had once again blocked his offer to buy the rights to her Noninvasive Prenatal Testing technology.

When his request for a meeting had been denied—not just once, but three different times—he'd gone with Plan B and asked Raine to pose as a prospective test subject to get inside information. It had been her idea that they pretend to be a married couple so he could get a firsthand look. He'd agreed, but couldn't help worrying that she'd gotten the wrong idea.

Or that she was playing him.

God knew, he'd fallen for it before.

Now, his fingers tightened on the phone. "No more Mr. and Mrs. Phillips. She pegged me as a ringer." Which was almost a relief.

"Then why do you need me?" Raine asked.

Not wanting to worry her unnecessarily, he said, "Just meet me in the Boston General lobby as soon as you can, okay? And bring the garment bag from my office closet. I need a change of clothes."

He cut the connection before she could ask why. He started to head back to the hospital, but a hail brought him up short.

"Mr. Falco? Lieutenant?"

Erik turned at the once-familiar title. "Falco, please. Or Erik. I haven't been a cop for nearly eight years."

The two plainclothes detectives wore badges clipped to their belts and standard-issue shoulder holsters beneath their jackets. The younger of the two—who looked close to Erik's age of thirty-eight—wore a brown suit that complemented his brown hair and clean-cut good looks, while his partner, who was closer to sixty, with a droopy, almost fishlike face, wore washed-out blue.

Both suits were decent quality but off-the-rack, just as Erik's had been back when he was on the job, back before a woman and his own stupidity had killed a good man and cost Erik the use of his leg and the life he'd known.

The brown-haired cop said, "I'm Detective Reid Peters." He gestured to his older partner. "This is Sturgeon. We'd like to ask you a few questions."

Erik blocked a spear of resentful nostalgia for the cop-speak and leaned on his cane. "Fire away."

Peters pulled out a PDA. It was a few generations older and much lower quality than Erik's top-of-the-line pocket computer, but it was still a far cry from the spiral-bound notebooks of years past. The younger detective used a stylus to tap open a new file, then set the record function before he asked, "How well do you know the victim?"

"She's not a victim—it was an accident." Erik narrowed his eyes. "Wasn't it?"

The detectives didn't answer, letting their original question hang.

Erik's temper spiked a notch. "Don't give me the silent routine. I was on the job—you know that or you wouldn't have called me 'lieutenant.' So I'll make a deal…you tell me what you know and I tell you what I know. Otherwise, you can talk to my lawyers. I have an entire department full, and they'll enjoy running you around for weeks if I tell them to."

Peters shared a look with Sturgeon, the sort of nonverbal communication partners developed over many years of teamwork.

The sort of look that reminded Erik of his old partner, James Hadley. Jimmy.

After a moment the older detective shrugged. "It might not have been an accident. There's supposed to be a metal railing separating the construction site from the sidewalk. The contractor swears it was put in last week, but it's gone."

"Contractors lie," Erik said, having been stung on a few projects over the years. "Subcontractors cut corners. That doesn't say 'intentional' to me."

But his instincts jangled. The sluiceway had opened at precisely the wrong moment. When he'd looked at the cement truck cab moments later, the driver had been gone, the door hanging open.

Peters stared at him for a long moment as though assessing him. Finally he nodded. "Have a look at this." He led them back through the police line, to the place where Meg had fallen through.

Erik took one look at the wooden railing and cursed bitterly. The panel had been neatly sawn through.

"So let me ask you." Peters tucked the PDA into his pocket, giving an illusion of off-the-record, though he hadn't turned off the recording feature. "Who was the target here? Boston General, Meg Corning…or you?"

Chapter Three

Raine knocked on the door to Meg's office almost an hour later, still looking polished and professional. Beautiful.

In comparison, Meg felt like a train wreck. Jemma had managed to find her a T-shirt to wear under a set of green scrubs, along with a pair of gym shoes, but that had been the extent of scroungeable spare clothes.

Meg was itchy and uncomfortable, and beginning to wish she'd taken that trip to the ER and from there gone home.

But she'd wanted to speak with Raine personally. The dark-haired beauty might work for FalcoTechno, she might have come to the lab under false pretenses, but she'd inadvertently made herself one of Meg's patients. Besides, whatever she'd done, she was a human being.

A woman. An expectant mother.

Meg waved her in. "Have a seat, Ms. Montgomery. I need to talk to you about something."

"If it's about what Erik and I did this morning, I'm sorry. I didn't mean—"

"It's not about that," Meg interrupted. "It's about the blood sample you gave us. There's a problem."

The bloom in the other woman's cheeks drained to pasty white, then took on a hot flush. "With the pregnancy?"

She didn't call it *the baby*. She called it *the pregnancy*. That, in Meg's clinical experience, was a telling detail. But this wasn't a counseling session, so she focused on the information that could save Raine's life. "It's not just the pregnancy. Our genetic screen revealed that you carry two gene mutations that put you at a high risk for developing blood clots in your arms and legs, or having a stroke or heart attack."

Meg had long ago learned that the blunt delivery was usually best in these cases. Just get it out there and deal with it.

"The pregnancy increases all of these risks exponentially. In addition, you have an increased risk of miscarriage—it's your body's way of trying to protect you from the other problems. There's good news, though—we can put you on supportive therapy starting now. If you're on interferon gamma and a strict monitoring program for the duration of the pregnancy, your chances are very good."

Raine moaned, a low exhalation of air that carried shock and fear. Her face reflected a shifting gamut of emotions, but she didn't say anything. Just clasped her hands in her lap and breathed deeply.

Tears glistened in her eyes.

"Is there someone you'd like to call?" Meg asked. "A family member, perhaps? I'll be happy to give you some privacy, if that would help."

But Raine shook her head. "No. No family."

"Your boss, then?" Meg realized she'd been petty to order Erik away from the lab. He and Raine might not be married, but she'd definitely sensed a connection between the two.

And why did the thought bring a twinge?

"No." Raine shook her head, took a deep breath, and lifted her chin. "I can handle this on my own."

But there was a faint quiver in her voice, and she looked as though a finger tap could knock her over.

"I'll have one of my people take you down to Admissions and start the paperwork. We'll need you to stay here for a day or so. After that, we can do the treatments on an outpatient basis."

Raine nodded slowly. "Fine. Of course."

Though the other woman had lied to her, and worked for the enemy, Meg's heart ached in sympathy.

God, she hated this part of the job.

She rose, detoured around the desk and leaned down to touch Raine's arm. "We'll take good care of you. I promise."

Swallowing what sounded like a sob, Raine nodded. "Thank you."

Meg led her out to the lab reception area. Jemma was away from her desk, but she saw Max's silhouette just inside the lab. She touched Raine's arm. "Wait here."

She pushed through the lab doors. "Max, I need you to do me a favor."

The big, dark-haired man set his lab notebook aside. "Sure, boss. What's up?"

"Remember those clotting factor and Factor V Leiden mutations you found the other day?" She jerked her head in the direction of the door. "She's out in the lobby, and pretty freaked out—with good reason. She didn't want me to call anyone, so can you take her down to Admissions and help expedite wherever you can? I think she could use somebody on her side right now."

Max nodded. "Of course." He rose, shucked off his lab coat to reveal jeans and a heavy flannel shirt, and headed for the lobby.

When he was gone, Jemma's voice spoke from behind Meg. "Bad idea, boss."

Meg turned, startled. "What?"

"Sending Max off with her. You're going to trigger his DIDS."

"His *what?*"

"Damsel In Distress Syndrome. That's what we call it behind his back, anyway." Jemma shrugged, but her eyes were clouded with faint worry. "Max is big and tough and mean-looking, but he's a sucker for a pretty woman with a sad story. Classic knight-on-a-white-horse mentality. If she doesn't watch out, he'll try to rescue her."

"I didn't know." Meg stared out into the now empty lobby. "Should I call him back?"

"Too late now. And besides, who knows? Maybe

it'll work out for him this time. She looks like she could use someone to lean on right now."

"True enough." Figuring what was done was done, and the important thing was getting Raine started on the life-saving therapy, Meg headed back to her office. But as she packed to leave for the day and tasted cement dust at the back of her throat, she was plagued by a faint sense of resentment that nobody ever volunteered to rescue her.

Or rather, someone had, but he was no white knight.

More like a sapphire-eyed devil intent on taking over her life's work.

MEG SLEPT POORLY that night, haunted by dreams of suffocation. Near 2:00 a.m., she gave up, snapped on her bedside lamp and read until dawn.

She was at the lab early, wearing the high-cut burnt-orange suit she only hauled out when she needed to remind herself that she was smart enough and tough enough to deal with whatever was going wrong.

Jemma met her at the door. "Cage wants you in his office, ASAP."

Meg cursed. She wasn't ready to meet with the head administrator before she'd even had her second hit of coffee. But with her work in a state of legal flux, she couldn't afford to ignore the summons. She took the elevator up from the fifth floor to the tenth and pushed through the door to Cage's office without knocking. "Sorry I'm late. I was discussing some extremely promising results with—"

She broke off and her stomach dipped to her toes.

She'd expected to see Zach Cage, the darkly handsome ex-major league pitcher who had taken over the reins of a troubled Boston General some three years earlier. She hadn't expected to see Erik Falco, wearing another dark gray suit and lighter gray shirt, this time with a vivid blue tie that picked up the cobalt in his eyes.

Worse, before the door had shut behind Meg, it opened again to admit a thin-hipped woman in her early forties with short, dark hair and piercing eyes. Annette Foulke, the nontenured Assistant Director of the Biochemistry Department at Thrace University, was Meg's equal in the hospital's hierarchy and had been anything but subtle in her efforts to block Meg from being voted tenure.

As far as Annette was concerned, the position should be hers.

Gritting her teeth as Annette sat primly beside Falco, Meg turned to Zach Cage, who sat behind his large, efficiently cluttered desk. "I didn't expect the Spanish Inquisition."

"Nobody expects the Spanish Inquisition," Falco said. His lips twitched briefly, and she had to give him points for knowing his *Monty Python*.

But all humor fled when Cage gestured her to the remaining empty chair. "Sit. We need to talk about what happened yesterday, and what we're going to do about it. Annette is here because she's the head of the hospital ethics committee. Mr. Falco is here to represent his interests."

Meg winced. Oh, hell. Somehow they'd figured

out that Max had used Raine's DNA for an unauthorized test. She sat, but stayed forward in her chair as she said, "If we hadn't done that genetic screen, the patient wouldn't have been identified as having—"

Cage held up a hand. "I'm not talking about your patients, Dr. Corning. I'm talking about what happened yesterday at the construction site."

Meg frowned and played it cool, as though she hadn't dreamed of the fact that she'd almost died. "It was an accident. I'm fine."

"It wasn't an accident," Cage said quietly. He tapped a file folder on his desk. "The permanent railing was removed and somebody sawed through the temporary wood railing. The police have ruled it sabotage. They want to talk to you as soon as we're done here."

"But I—" Meg's breath whooshed out as his words caught up with her brain. "*Sabotage?* Impossible!"

But she flashed back on the jostling crowd. She'd pushed through the pedestrians near the construction site, called Erik's name, reached for him—

And she'd been bumped from behind. Hard.

"We think the hospital may have been targeted by someone who doesn't approve of the new wing. This is the latest in a string of problems with the new construction," Cage said. "When I took over, it seemed reasonable to continue building the Gabney Wing, though of course, under a new name."

Meg nodded, brain spinning with too much information, too many questions. "Of course." She knew that the previous head administrator, Leo Gabney, had put the project into motion before being fired. Though the construction was a major undertaking, so much of the preliminary work had already been done—and paid for—that it had made fiscal sense for the hospital to break ground.

That had been eighteen months ago, and broken ground was almost all they had to show for it now. Broken ground and some cement forms.

Cage shifted in his chair, face creasing with regret. "This added delay—on top of cost overruns—puts me in a tough position. Gabney left us with debts, and the plans weren't nearly as complete as they appeared at first. We probably shouldn't have gone ahead with the project, but now that we've started building—and made promises to the clinicians and researchers who are lined up to use the space—we can't turn back."

Meg's heart picked up a beat as she realized where this was going. "We've already nixed the idea of selling off the NPT technology to cover the construction costs. We agreed that the long-term licensing income outweighed the short term gain from a sale."

"That was before someone tried to kill you," Erik said bluntly.

"That's ridiculous!" She shot to her feet. "You heard what Cage said—the construction project was the target. I was just in the wrong place at the wrong time."

"Detectives Peters and Sturgeon aren't so sure," Falco countered. "Are you willing to bet your life that they're wrong?"

She glared at him. "You set this up, didn't you? Cage turned down your repeated offers to buy my patents, so you came up with this…this *farce* to sway him. Well, do you know what? It won't fly. I wouldn't sell my work to FalcoTechno if it were—"

"Sit down, Dr. Corning." Cage's voice cracked whip-sharp. When she'd taken her seat, his tone softened with regret. "I know you oppose the sale and I know why. I even agree with you to an extent. But I can't let that dictate hospital policy. With all the cost overruns, we need the money. FalcoTechno has made a more than generous offer, far exceeding what the other companies have—"

Annette broke in. "Excuse me for interrupting, but I'm confused as to why you asked me here. I thought you wanted my opinion on a matter of ethics."

"Not quite." Cage nodded to Falco, who leaned down and lifted a briefcase off the floor. He popped the top and withdrew a fat stack of papers as the head administrator said, "I need a committee head to witness any deal over fifty million dollars. Your schedule was open."

Annette stood. "Next time, ask before you decide my schedule is open. I was in the middle of an important experiment. Get someone else to do your paperwork."

She stalked out, tension humming in her wake.

Meg expected the head administrator to call her back with a reprimand. Instead he rubbed the back of his neck. "God, she's a pain. And she wonders why she keeps getting passed over for promotion."

Seeing a slim opening, Meg stood and placed herself square in front of the administrator's desk. "If you can't do the paperwork right now, give me a chance. I'll license out the NPT technology to a smaller company, but make sure that Boston General keeps managing interest. Surely you can see the value in that?" She had to protect her work, protect the patients who would benefit from the noninvasive prenatal testing. She lowered her voice so only Cage could hear. "We've talked about this. I have to make sure the technology is used correctly."

There was too much potential for disaster.

Cage looked at her for a long, considering moment before he said, "The sabotage could have been aimed at you, not the hospital. We're talking about a ton of money here. If someone's trying to kill the deal by eliminating the driving force behind the technology, then putting the sale through sooner than later will keep you safe."

"Nobody asked you to protect me," she said. "I'm tougher than you think. Don't let Falco talk you into believing something that suits his purposes. I'm not the target. If anything, someone's finally decided to sabotage Leo Gabney's white elephant of a construction project. Shut it down and be done with it, but don't shut me down. I can make the licensing work for both of us. I swear it."

The head administrator stared at her for so long,

his expression so closed, that she expected him to say no. When he nodded reluctantly, she nearly wept with relief. "Okay," he said. "You've got a month to pull together a profitable licensing proposal that's ready for my signature, with a company that's willing to pay for the technology but let us retain veto rights on development."

"My offer will be revoked once I walk out that door," Falco said smoothly. "And you know damn well it's better than you're going to get anywhere else."

Meg turned on him. "You want the NPT technology? Then license it."

He shook his head. "No thanks, I don't share control. I'll buy your work, but now, not a month from now."

Cage snorted. "Don't try to outnegotiate a negotiator, Falco. If you want the deal badly enough, you'll wait. Give us one week."

"One week," Erik said, his expression suggesting that was what he'd wanted all along. "I can wait that long to own my new technology."

Meg's smile held an edge. "You'll be waiting longer than that." She headed for the door. "Excuse me, I have calls to make."

As she strode down the hall toward the elevator, she was already running through the options in her head. A week was better than nothing, but she was going to have trouble licensing out a technology that hadn't even passed full beta testing yet.

No, that wasn't true, she acknowledged inwardly.

There were a half dozen companies—Falco's included—slavering to get their hands on the NPT technology. But it would be more difficult to find one willing to sign the agreement she had in mind, which would restrict the scope of the license to prenatal testing alone.

She and Cage had planned to patent the other aspects of the work and sit on them.

The world wasn't ready for every facet of the NPT process. Not yet. Maybe not ever.

A door opened and closed behind her, and Falco's voice called, "Dr. Corning. Meg, wait!"

She stabbed the elevator call button, hoping to escape before he reached her. But his hitching stride ate up the distance between them, and the glowing elevator light stalled on the eighth floor.

He stopped beside her, loomed over her. "Not so fast. You and I are going to be spending some quality time together."

She glared. "I don't think so. You heard Cage. I have seven days."

The elevator doors finally whooshed open, too late to do her any good. She set her teeth as they stepped into the empty car together. Falco hit the button for the ground-floor lobby before he said, "Yeah, and I'm going to stick very close to you for those seven days. Let's just say I've learned my lesson when it comes to trusting women."

Fuming, Meg turned on him. "How dare you insinuate that I would ever—"

The elevator jolted, throwing her against him. She gasped in alarm and reached up to push away from him, winding up with both palms flat against his hard, masculine chest. She felt his heartbeat, quick like hers.

Something changed in his expression. "Look, I—"

A grating, popping noise drowned out his next words. A metallic pinging reverberated through the elevator car. The lights died.

And the floor dropped out from underneath them.

Chapter Four

Erik shouted and grabbed Meg. He tried to shield her with his body, but it was impossible. The danger was all around them.

The elevator floor barely pressed against his feet as they fell, giving a sense of weightlessness even as nausea jammed at the back of his throat.

He twisted, still holding Meg against his chest, and slapped the red Emergency Stop button beneath the main panel.

Nothing happened.

He punched the red button harder. "Engage, damn it!"

The brakes locked. Metal screamed and sparks leaped up through the carpeted floor, which jolted and slowed its descent.

Unbalanced by the sudden change in inertia, Erik crashed to the floor. Meg landed atop him, driving the breath from his lungs.

"We're still moving!" she shouted in his ear, panic cranking her voice to a shriek.

"Hang on!" Erik tightened his arms around her and tucked her face beside his as the grating squeal of metal-on-metal intensified. The howling sound reverberated in his skull until—

Crash!

The impact slammed him flat. His head bounced off the carpeted floor and rebounded into Meg's shoulder. He cut his lip between his teeth and her collarbone, and tasted blood. Her body dug into his and then sprawled away as a final crashing noise ripped through the small space.

Then the cacophony died, leaving a strange, heavy silence broken only by the strident ring of alarms. A small, battery-powered emergency light provided wan illumination.

They'd hit bottom. They'd survived.

Erik let the knowledge work its way through him, partway expecting relief. He found anger instead. Red, bloody anger.

That was no accident.

It wasn't until he heard the words echo in the noisy silence that he realized he'd said it out loud.

Beside him, sprawled half over him, Meg moaned and stirred. Her elbow jabbed him in the ribs, and when she rolled off him, she shoved her knee against his bad leg, sending shooting sparks of pain to join the dizzy ache of impact.

Erik buried the wince and turned to look at her. "You okay?"

She levered herself to a seated position, then slumped back against the wall. Her orangey suit and tall black boots still looked as professional as they had when she'd first stepped into Cage's office. But her red-gold hair had fallen from its slick knot, making her look less unapproachable. More vulnerable.

She shifted experimentally before she said, "Everything works, if that's what you're asking. But no, I'm not okay. We were just…we just…" Her full lower lip trembled until she bit it and mastered the half-formed tears. "Sorry. I'm fine. How about you?"

The sirens cut out then, leaving a chilly silence that was soon broken by thumps overhead.

Far overhead.

"No broken bones, and I'll settle for that under the circumstances." Erik grabbed his cane and used it to push himself up off the floor, which was tilted beneath them. He put a steadying hand on the wall and reached up to bang on the ceiling of the elevator car, where a body-size panel hung slightly askew. "Looks like this'll be our way out. You want me to boost you up, or would you rather wait for an official rescue?"

The thumping noises increased overhead as Meg's eyes met his. "What if that's not the official rescue?" she asked quietly.

Then *we're sitting ducks*, he thought. With the elevator lying at the bottom of the shaft, there was no way they were getting the main doors open. It was out the top or nothing.

But the question remained… What if whoever had engineered the fall was up there waiting?

He saw understanding in her eyes, a grim sort of fatalism that clashed with his impression of the woman. It made him wonder if there was more to her than the academic exterior she projected. His investigators had mentioned she'd been a bit of a hellion in her younger years, and concluded she'd outgrown the risk-taking behavior. Her quiet calm made him wonder whether she'd retained more of her skydiving, bungee-jumping past than she let on.

Or, his suspicious side prompted, *maybe she's like Celia. Maybe this is all part of a plan.*

"Boost me up," she ordered.

He stared for a moment, as her image merged in his mind with that of another woman, lighter in coloring except for the red slash of her painted lips.

Then he shook his head to banish the image. Celia was gone for twenty-to-life and had no place in his head. Meg Corning was nothing like her.

Nothing at all.

"I'll go first," he said finally. He motioned her to the corner as the banging continued overhead. "Watch yourself."

"You want a boost?"

He bit back the automatic retort. "I've got it." He poked the cane up with more force than necessary, sending the panel clattering out of the way. Then he wedged the rubber-tipped end on the metal handrail that looped around the elevator car, used the cane as leverage, jumped as high as he could manage, and grabbed the edge of the escape hatch with his free hand. Cursing with the effort, he dragged his upper body through the opening one-handed, then pulled the cane up after him.

It wasn't much of a weapon, but it was all he had left.

Exertion sang through his bloodstream, sending his pulse into his ears. A quick glance showed him a lighted rectangle some twenty feet above, stark contrast to the darkness of the elevator shaft, which was lined with metal, cement and thick cables.

A human figure stood silhouetted in the doorway. Another clung to the side of the shaft, maybe fifteen feet away.

Erik stayed silent, though there was little hope of avoiding detection. With one muscle-popping surge of effort, he scrambled to his feet until he was standing atop the ruined elevator car with his cane in his fist, a weak defense against the dark shadow that dropped down the final feet separating them, landed heavily atop the elevator car, and clasped his shoulder.

"You're okay. Thank God."

Relief laced through Erik. It was Zach Cage. Rescue, not attack.

"What happened?" the hospital administrator asked, then cursed. "Never mind. Dumb question. Is Meg hurt?"

"She's rattled," Erik said as a coil of rope snaked down from above and the crackle of radio traffic announced the arrival of official personnel. "And frankly, so am I. You know what this means, don't you?"

Cage nodded grimly. "The hospital isn't the

target. These so-called accidents are focused on one of you guys. Question is, which one?"

"I don't know," Erik admitted, "but I'm damn well going to find out."

THE NEXT HALF HOUR passed in a blur of firefighters and paramedics that seemed all too familiar to Meg.

Two near-death experiences in two days. How was she supposed to deal with that?

She didn't know, but as she sat alone at a conference table in a bare, faintly cool room deep within the Chinatown police station, she gave herself a stern talking-to. "You've bungee jumped off a bridge. You've skydived. You've pedaled bikes off the sides of cliffs. Hell, you even base-jumped off a skyscraper once. You used to get a rush out of stuff like this."

So why were her hands shaking? Why was her stomach knotted and why were her knees doing a fair impression of Jell-O?

Because those rushes were years in the past. And because she'd chosen the dangers. Over the past forty-eight hours, danger had come looking for her, and all she wanted to do was to run home and hide. She hadn't signed up for this. She was a researcher, damn it, not a contestant on some freaky reality show where people volunteered to be buried in cement or dropped down elevator shafts in an effort to win a million dollars.

Even as she gritted her teeth on the thought, the door opened, admitting Erik Falco and the two detectives who'd earlier introduced themselves as

Peters and Sturgeon. They were easy to tell apart—Peters was the handsome, athletic one. Sturgeon had that Mr. Limpet thing going on. And Falco…

Hell, she didn't know what to think about him. Most of the time, he leaned on that two-toned cane as though he was utterly dependent on its support, scowling to let the world know he hated every minute of it. He didn't want sympathy, but he also didn't seem comfortable in his own skin, regardless of the expensive clothes and tasteful haircut. But once or twice she'd seen flashes of something else, like when he'd rescued her from the cement or shielded her body with his during the crash. Then, he'd seemed to grow bigger. Taller. Meaner.

In those moments, he'd made her feel safe.

But now…now he stumped into the room and dropped heavily into a chair opposite her at the round conference table. His handsome face hardened into a glare, as though everything was somehow her fault.

Meg found herself bristling. "Don't give me that look. If you hadn't insisted on pursuing a deal I have no intention of making, none of this would have happened."

Detective Peters paused in the act of setting up his PDA to record the conversation and glanced at them. "What deal?"

"Falco here wants to buy my patents, and can't get it through his thick skull that NPT isn't for sale," Meg said. "Not to him, anyway."

Maybe she shouldn't snipe at a man who'd let her

use his body as a landing pad when their elevator crashed. But business was business.

Falco smiled at her with an expression that showed lots of teeth and very little warmth. "Like I said before, call me Erik. We're going to be working closely together this week, so there's no need to stand on formality." He glanced at the detectives. "Unfortunately for Meg, she doesn't hold veto power over the hospital's decision. Unless she's able to come up with a licensor willing to accept her terms—highly unlikely—the deal will go through one week from today."

His use of her first name struck a chord she wasn't entirely comfortable with, and had her hissing out a breath. A week. He was going to be dogging her tracks for the next seven days, probably ambushing her attempts to gather investors.

She didn't know much about Erik Falco, but she had a pretty good idea he wouldn't give up easily. Hell, he'd been working to get the deal done for months, and it hadn't been until the last few days that Cage had begun yielding to the hospital's growing financial pressures.

Come to think of it… "None of this started until Cage agreed in principle to FalcoTechno's offer," Meg said slowly. "What if someone's trying to sabotage the deal?"

"If that's the case, I expect you'll track them down and offer to help." Erik's grimace suggested he was being sarcastic, but he continued. "It is possible, though. Several other companies are in the running for the NPT technology."

"Nobody's in the running," Meg snapped. Her eyes itched, her brain felt as if it were stuffed with cotton batting and she was perilously close to tears. She bit her lip until the urge receded. "But I think it's a valid hypothesis. If—and this is only hypothetical—if we agree that Erik and I were the target of these attacks, then our attacker could be someone trying to tank the deal."

Detective Sturgeon flattened an index card on the table in front of him, apparently eschewing his partner's technology. "Names?"

Erik flicked his fingers to dismiss the question. "I'll work that end of things."

Meg expected the detectives to rip a layer off him for the I've-got-money-I'm-above-your-rules attitude.

Instead Peters said, "We'd appreciate it—on an unofficial basis, of course. But I'll still need a list of everyone who might have reason to want you or Dr. Corning dead."

The last word sent a chilly spear through her midsection and she fought a shiver.

"I've got a few names," Erik said, not sounding particularly upset by the fact. "How about you, Doc?"

"There's nobody," she said, pressing her fingers to her temples, where stress and nerves pounded in an increasing rhythm. "I can't imagine anyone wanting to hurt me."

"When the NPT technology is released, there's going to be a big shift in the open market," Erik pointed out. "Jobs'll be lost. Cash equity is going to move around. Money is a powerful motive."

Meg scowled, hearing the sentiment echo in her father's voice. *For some people, money is the best motive.*

Even as a young girl, she'd known he meant her mother. Though many years and a few awkward meetings with the woman who had birthed her had given Meg some perspective, the fact remained. Her mother had cared less for her family than she had for things that couldn't be bought on an academic's salary.

The door opened and a dark-haired cop stuck his head into the room, interrupting. "Detectives? I think you'll want to see this."

Sturgeon rose and followed the man out. Peters shut down his PDA and said, "Wait here, I'll see what's up."

But before he cleared the room, Sturgeon was back. The older detective spoke quietly in his partner's ear. Peters stiffened and cursed before turning to Meg and Erik. "We'll have to continue this later. We'll be in touch."

Erik rose. "A break?"

"Yes, but not in your case," Sturgeon answered on his way out the door.

Peters paused and leveled a finger at Erik. "Don't go Lone Ranger. You're not on the job anymore. Find out what you can from the sidelines and leave the heavy lifting to us."

"I don't have much of a choice," Erik said, leaning on the two-toned cane.

But Peters's eyes darkened speculatively before he let the door swing shut in his wake, leaving Meg to think he'd noticed, too, how Falco's reliance on the cane seemed to change with his mood.

Or maybe that was her imagination, brought on by too much stress and her unwilling awareness of the man.

She gathered her things and rose. "I guess I'll head back to the lab."

Surprise flashed in his dark eyes. "You're not going home? Surely, you can take the rest of the day off after the morning you've had."

"Sorry, no. I have work to do."

The truth was that she didn't want to go home.

It had been hard enough the night before, when she'd checked the doors and windows twice and still hadn't felt completely safe. Now, knowing that the accident with the cement hadn't been an accident at all, she didn't imagine the wooden storm door with the single-barrel bolt would feel any safer. She was better off in the lab, which had levels of security between her and the outside world.

"I'll walk you over."

Though part of her wanted to tell him to leave her the hell alone and go back to his own life, she sucked it up and nodded. "Fine." Then she slanted him a look. "The question is, am I safer with or without you?"

Though the question could have too many layers, he grimaced and took it at face value. "I wish I knew. If I'm the target, then you're safer without me. If you're the target, then you're safer—at least marginally—with me. If we're both being targeted…hell, who knows? We're watching each other's backs or we're making it easier on them by leaving a single target. Hard to tell."

His answer was anything but reassuring, but Meg appreciated the honesty. She jerked her head toward the door. "Okay. Let's go."

They were both tense as they left the Chinatown police station and turned toward Washington Street. It would take longer for them to find a cab and fight the lunchtime traffic than it would to walk the four short blocks back to Boston General. But walking left them out in the open.

Unprotected.

Meg wasn't sure whether the creeping feeling that descended the back of her neck and set up residence in her stomach was the power of suggestion or not. As they waited to cross Washington Street, she glanced over her shoulder, looking for…damn, she didn't know what she was looking for.

"Relax," Erik said quietly from beside her. "I've got your back."

The light turned then and the pedestrian sign went the white of "walk." As they started across, she glanced at his stern, set profile. "Who's got yours?"

"I don't need anyone to get my back. I'm a tough guy." His lips twisted in a self-deprecating smile as he walked with a heavy hitch in his step. "Or not."

But Meg was starting to see the holes in his act. She remembered the detectives' attitudes toward him—part caution, part camaraderie. "You were a cop, weren't you?"

His step faltered, then resumed as they reached the other curb and turned up the final block to the hospital. "A long time ago." His cynical smile twisted tighter. "Why? Does that make you feel safer? It shouldn't. I've been a civilian for the past eight years."

"What happened?"

"It's not important," he said flatly. "It has nothing to do with the attacks."

They reached the hospital and crossed the main atrium in a tense silence that told her there would be no more small talk.

She paused at the stairs, where the door was propped open and the foot traffic was unusually heavy. She glanced over at the elevator lobby and her stomach tightened at the sight of crime scene tape and cops.

"Let's take the—" She broke off and shook her head. "Never mind. Sorry. We can take the other set of elevators."

"I can climb stairs," he said sharply. "It's a cane, not a wheelchair. You don't need to make a big deal about it."

"Why not? You do," Meg snapped, irritated with him, with the whole rotten situation. Then she blew out a breath. "Sorry."

"Don't be." He turned away and headed for the stairs, back straight and stiff, walking almost normally.

She hurried to catch up and reached to grab his shoulder. "Wait."

The heat of him radiated through the material of his shirt, and his muscles were tense and bunched beneath her touch. He stopped and turned, forcing her to drop her hand. His dark brows were drawn low over his piercing eyes, and his expression held something dark and forbidding. "What?"

She forced herself to stand up to him when she wanted to fall back a step. "Look, I said I was sorry. It's just…this is weird for me. I don't like it."

His lips twisted. "I'm not a big fan of attempted murder, either, especially when I'm the target."

She blew out a breath. "It's not just that. It's this whole situation. You're not actually planning on shadowing me for the next six and a half days, are you? I mean, I don't spend that much time with *anyone*. You hardly know me."

"I know enough," he said. "Meg Corning, daughter of Felicity and Robert Corning, divorced. Your mother is married to the president of TCR Pharmaceuticals. Your father, who raised you from the age of five when your mother left, won a Nobel Prize a few years ago for his early work on gene therapy.

"In an act of teenage rebellion you left home at eighteen and hitched your way around the globe, working your way from one extreme sport to the next." His eyes were unreadable as he continued. "You had at least two serious relationships during that time—one with a skydiver, one with a scientist, neither lasting more than six months. You resurfaced in grad school at twenty-five and swore you'd prove that fetal cells circulate in the maternal bloodstream. It sounded like another extreme sport, only extreme science this time around. But to everyone's surprise, you actually succeeded, and hit the cover of *Science* magazine with your first major paper on Noninvasive Prenatal Testing. Since then, you've settled down and focused on perfecting the technique."

When he paused, she gritted her teeth. "Are you done?"

"Not quite." Now he looked at her, and those piercing eyes seemed to cut through to her core. "You live alone in a town house near Beacon Hill, you don't date, and you joined a gym last winter. You attend yoga classes three times a week and climbing classes every Friday night."

A chill worked its way through her. "Are you trying to tick me off or freak me out?"

He looked away. "Maybe a bit of both. I want to make sure you understand how easy it is to get that sort of information if you don't mind paying."

Meg stalled as fear tangled around resentment in her chest. Resentment won. "You've made it clear that you don't mind paying, whether or not something's for sale." She frowned. "I don't suppose you want to return the favor and give me the thirty-second version of Erik Falco? Since you're threatening to shadow me for the next six-plus days, it seems only fair that I know something about you."

His expression closed suddenly, becoming blank.

Impenetrable. "What I want known is public record. The rest is private."

"Which tells me exactly nothing."

He took a breath and glanced around, a not-so-subtle reminder that they were standing in the Boston General elevator lobby. "Let's go upstairs."

"Let's not," she countered, knowing she was being petty, but damn tired of letting circumstances push her around. "I'd like to know who's looking over my shoulder."

He gritted his teeth. "Fine. My name is Erik Charles Falco. I'm thirty-eight, I'm single, and I'm looking to stay that way."

"There you are!" a female voice broke in, and suddenly Raine Montgomery was between them. Dark hollows beneath her eyes spoke of a sleepless night, but her expression brightened when she ranged herself beside Erik and touched his sleeve. "Are you coming up with me?"

He stared at her for a moment as though he barely recognized her. "Yeah, sure, I'm headed—" He broke off with a telling glance at Meg. "Of course."

The three of them climbed the stairs to the fifth floor while Erik briefed Raine on the elevator "accident." The other woman made all the right noises of fear and distress, but kept herself firmly wedged between Meg and Erik.

I'm single, he'd said, *and I'm looking to stay that way.*

But as Meg watched Raine guide him away and keep him carefully engaged, she realized that singlehood was as good as gone if Erik's vice president of pharmaceuticals had anything to say about it.

And that thought annoyed her to no end.

THE DETECTIVES APPEARED in the lab a few hours later to continue their questioning. As he sat in Meg's office, listening to Peters ask her about her business contacts and ex-employees, Erik's attention was split.

Part of him analyzed the information like the businessman he had become, mentally reviewing the files he'd amassed on the major players at Boston General and Thrace University, and considering whether the threats could be coming from an enemy of Falco-Techno. Part of him listened with the ears of the cop he had once been. But still another part of him was too aware of Meg, of the way she caught her lower lip between her teeth before answering each question, as though this was an exam she was determined to pass.

He was aware of the curve at the side of her neck, where her red-gold hair hung down to shade her face ever so slightly, and he was aware that she looked at him sidelong when she didn't think he was paying attention, as if she was trying to figure him out.

Or was that all calculated?

The part of him that noticed her scent wanted to believe that she was genuine. But a pulse of pain—phantom, perhaps, but real nonetheless—in his leg was a living reminder of a fatal summer day when he'd learned one important lesson.

When a beautiful woman who has every reason to hate you shows interest instead, she has an agenda.

"I've racked my brain," Meg said, returning Erik's attention to the detectives' questions. "I've come up with a few other scientists who were fairly vocal in their efforts to disprove NPT." She grabbed a pen and scribbled three names. "The top two lost fairly major drug-company funding after I made my announcement. They weren't pleased." She grimaced, indicating that was an understatement, but continued. "Still, I can't imagine them thinking that hurting me would fix anything. They're smart, rational people."

Erik snorted. "Rationality has a tendency to fly out the window when large sums of money are involved."

She glanced at him. "Which is why I think that it's much more likely we'll find our man on your list. Industry attracts the scientists who are more—" she paused before saying "—aggrandizing. Self-centered. In it for the quick buck."

Erik tipped his head. "Are those your words or your father's?"

Her eyes darkened and her mouth compressed to a thin line. "Don't believe everything your investigators told you."

"Believe me, I make my own opinions. I just like to collect all the available data before I do," Erik said.

"Getting back to the matter at hand," Detective Peters broke in, "our reason for coming here this morning was twofold." He nodded at Meg's scribbled list. "We wanted to see if you'd come up with any possible suspects. But we also wanted to update you on our investigation."

Erik stiffened, knowing damn well that self-respecting cops usually tried their hardest to keep civilians *out* of the loop until they had something definitive. That meant that either they were extending him an ex-cop's courtesy or they had something major to report.

The grim expression on Sturgeon's jowly face suggested the latter.

"We had an engineer look at the elevators. There were remote-controlled charges wired to different cables in each of the shafts. You two got lucky," Peters said. "If you'd picked either of the other cars, the emergency brakes wouldn't have kicked in near the bottom."

Oh, hell, Erik thought. "How much of a radius did the remote receiver have?"

"A few hundred yards, maybe less," Peters answered.

That drew a gasp from Meg. "Someone triggered it from *inside* the hospital?"

"They had to be inside to plant the charges in the first place," Erik reminded her. "And don't forget that someone was in the cement truck the other day to drop that load on top of you. This wasn't the first time he—or she—was near us."

The truck's real driver had been found between the skids of a nearby front-end loader. He'd been attacked from behind, knocked unconscious and

gagged, and hadn't been able to describe his assail-
ant. But knowing that their attacker had been right
near them inside the hospital, waiting to see which
elevator they would board, which charge to detonate,
added to the sense of invasion.

"Does the hospital have video surveillance on the
hallways?" Erik asked.

"In the hallways and lobbies." Peters lifted one
shoulder in a negative half shrug. "Not in the elevator
shafts, though, or in the access areas."

"In other words, we don't have a picture of our saboteur," Erik said flatly. "Or if we do, there's no way
for us to identify him because there are hundreds, if
not thousands, of people in and out of the hospital
on a daily basis."

"Which leaves us where?" Meg demanded.
She'd gone pale and her fingers were knotted
together in her lap.

"Still working on it," Peters said. He glanced
between Erik and Meg. "Until we've got a better
idea of who and what we're looking for, I think we
need to assume that both of you are in danger." He
focused on Erik. "You carrying?"

"No," Erik answered flatly. "Not with my current
balance—or lack thereof."

The detective shifted uncomfortably. There was
little a cop hated more than being reminded of his
own mortality. His own potential for disaster.

"Don't worry," Erik said, glossing over the
awkward moment. "I'll keep a very close eye on
Dr. Corning."

"Who asked you to?" she scoffed. "I'm perfectly safe in the lab—have you seen how many codes it takes to get in here? Besides, I have work to do."

He shrugged. "I'll watch. Let's just say I'm looking to protect my investment."

More truthfully, he was looking to do everything in his power to make sure the sale happened. He already had people on the job. "Use whatever methods it takes," he'd said, and he'd meant it. There was no room for emotion or misgivings.

This was business.

Meg scowled. "I'm not letting you into the lab."

"Try keeping me out." He nodded toward the detectives, who were packing to leave. "You heard what they said. The saboteur could be anyone. Anywhere. Consider it two for the price of one—I protect you at the same time that I'm protecting my investment."

"And if you're the focus of the danger?"

He shrugged. "Then I look forward to meeting the bastard who's after me."

OUTSIDE THE HOSPITAL, Edward watched the detectives emerge and squint into the autumn sunlight that shone down on the sidewalks and thronging pedestrians. The younger of the pair nodded toward the deserted construction site, and the partners walked to the taped-off area where the bitch had fallen through.

No doubt they were looking for more evidence, but Edward wasn't concerned. The first plan had been a good one, clean and well-executed, only thwarted by sheer bad luck.

The second plan had been less successful. He still couldn't believe the elevator car had stopped short of the bottom.

There are no second chances in life, his mother used to say. *You have to get it right the first time or work to correct the mistakes.*

Edward wasn't exactly working to correct a mistake; he was ensuring that a larger mistake wouldn't come to pass.

Still, the same principles applied. Do it right the first time.

The first failure could be attributed to bad luck, the second to poor planning. Yet he was still free, still undiscovered. That very freedom gave him another opportunity to complete the task.

The bitch would die soon.

Chapter Five

Three days of relative quiet later, Meg sat in on Raine's interferon treatment and then retreated to her office to hit the phones.

It took her five calls to realize something was up. She would've realized it sooner, but she was distracted by Erik, who'd put Raine in a cab, returned to the lab and set up shop in a corner of her office with his laptop and cell phone.

She scowled at him, trying not to notice that today's suit was blue-gray, and his burgundy tie wasn't quite snug to his collar, giving him a more casual, approachable air.

Not that she was looking to approach him, of course. He was her enemy in the battle of the NPT licensing.

The executive assistant at Donoway Drugs came back on the phone line. "I'm sorry, Dr. Corning, he's tied up in a meeting." But she didn't sound one bit sorry. She sounded like she was lying through her teeth. "I'll have him call you the moment he's free."

Which, Meg realized as she disconnected the call, would be exactly never.

She glared at Erik, whose fingers flew on the compact keyboard of his laptop. "You called them, didn't you? You told them not to buy into my licensing offer. That's cheating."

"You're just mad that I got there before you did." He looked up at her, his eyes deceptively mild. "Or did you think I was going to pull my punches because you've sent me a few 'come hither' looks and flipped your hair over the past few days?"

Anger flared low in her gut, directed at herself as well as him. She'd tried not to look, but hadn't been able to help herself. It had been a long while since she'd been cooped up in close quarters with a man that she—like it or not—found attractive. She'd only hoped he hadn't noticed.

Obviously he had.

"Damn it," she said to the room at large, not sure whether she was talking to herself or him. She grabbed the phone, punched in a string of numbers and waited for it to ring through. When a female voice answered, she said, "Meg Corning here, returning your call. Do you have good news for me?"

There was a beat of startled silence on the other end. Meg muttered something under her breath. "Falco got to you, too, didn't he? What did he say?" She nodded and shot him a furious glare. "Mmm-hmm. Mmm-hmm. No, that doesn't surprise me in the slightest… What? Yes, I agree that it certainly sounds like blackmail—or at least undue influence.

Would you be willing to write that up and have it no-
tarized for me?" She nodded and flashed him a
gotcha grin. "Perfect. I'll owe you one... What? Yes,
this definitely gets you priority when the licensing
deal goes through." She punched the disconnect
button with a cry of victory and pointed the phone
at Falco. "How do you like that?"

With no change in expression, he tipped his head
toward the open doorway. "You might want to
reassure your assistant that you haven't lost your
mind."

Meg winced and looked out into the lobby, where
Jemma sat at her desk, typing furiously, a hot blush
staining her cheeks.

Busted.

"And when bluffing," Erik said mildly, "might I
suggest that next time you make sure to dial an
outside line?"

"Hell." She stared at the phone, realizing she'd
given herself away by dialing the five digits of an
inside call rather than the ten-plus required to phone
any of her possible investors. "That was stupid."

He shrugged. "Beginner's mistake."

She remained staring at the phone, unwilling to
look at him, hating the strange tension that had snapped
into place between them. "Did you threaten everyone?"

There was a beat of silence before he said, "I don't
threaten, I advise. And yes, I advised most of the
companies interested in the NPT technology—those
not owned by FalcoTechno and its subsidiaries,

of course—that I would be grateful if they let your offer slide."

Numbness closed in on her. "And they agreed? What happened to marketplace competition?"

"If any of my competitors thought your offer was a good one, they'd go up against me in an instant. Since all you're offering is the opportunity to buy an extremely restrictive license without any development potential, they've been more than willing to give it a miss. Probably would've anyway."

"Baloney," she said. "The technique is going to revolutionize prenatal testing."

"True, but it could do so much more if the other aspects were developed."

An icy ball lodged in her belly. "Which is precisely why I don't want to lose control of the patents. The ethics are—"

"The ethics aren't the issue," he interrupted. He closed the laptop with a decisive click and turned the full force of his attention on her. The piercing intensity of his blue eyes chilled the ice inside her even further when he said, "Sure, some people will set off down the bioethics warpath the moment you say *stem cells,* but we're not talking about experimenting on embryos here. That's the whole point. We're talking about a blood sample."

The ice moved from her gut into her bloodstream as an uneasy suspicion formed in her brain. "No, we're not talking about it at all, because I'm going to find someone to license NPT on my terms, or else."

"Or else what?" he said, very calmly, almost dangerously calm, as though he were accusing her of planning something she hadn't even thought of.

The phone rang, making her jump. Her heart rate spiked at the thought that it might be an investor phoning her back. But no, it was an inside line. She eschewed the speakerphone in favor of privacy and lifted the handset. "This is Dr. Corning."

"It's Max. There's something I think you should see in the lab." A thread of excitement ran through his normally gruff voice, telling Meg it was something good.

"I'll be right there." She replaced the handset and glanced over to find that Erik hadn't returned to his computer. He was still looking at her. Watching her.

Judging her, though she didn't know what she'd been accused of.

A sizzle of frustration beat at the worry, but she said only, "You keep doing what you're doing. I'm needed in the lab."

He set the laptop aside and rose, leaning heavily on the cane and wincing. "What I'm doing is keeping an eye on you."

A momentary beat of empathy fled quickly in the face of irritation. "If you're protecting me from the person who may or may not be trying to kill us, then you don't need to follow me into my own lab. If I'm not safe there, where am I safe?" The starkness of the words brought an involuntary shudder and she quickly continued. "And if you're protecting your supposed future investment, then you should take a serious look at yourself in the mirror. That level of paranoia can't be healthy."

She expected his anger, even welcomed it on some level. His anger distanced him, made him seem less approachable than he'd been when they worked together in her office, quietly sharing space like longtime co-workers.

Or partners. Lovers.

And where had *that* thought come from?

Rattled, she headed for the lab, aware of Erik following at a distance, far enough away that she couldn't accuse him of breathing down her neck, even though that was exactly what it felt like.

When she bent over Max's fluorescent microscope she could almost feel the weight of Falco's gaze, but when she straightened to snap at him, he was half a room away, leaning against a wall.

Yet his eyes held a knowing gleam. Why? Because he sensed her ridiculously misplaced attraction and found it amusing? Or because he imagined a far more sinister motive for her glare?

"Did you see it?" Max demanded, gesturing to the fluoroscope, which held the results of his latest series of tests.

That was when Meg realized she'd been so preoccupied by thoughts of Erik that she hadn't even registered what she'd seen. "I'm sorry." She made a vague gesture. "I'm distracted."

It was day four of her seven-day timeline. There hadn't been any new attacks.

But she hadn't made any progress on the licensing, either, save for a vague promise of a "maybe" from Genticor after she forced herself to go through her mother's second husband, and a "we'll look into it" from Pentium Pharmaceuticals.

Max grimaced, but his voice wasn't as gruff as usual when he said, "You should take off early. Do something nice for yourself. Go home and have a bubble bath or something."

She nearly snorted at the idea—she couldn't remember ever thinking of a bubble bath as a first line of defense against stress.

Earlier in her life, when she'd been upset—and that was most of the time—she'd tested the boundaries between danger and safety. Windsong had soothed the jagged edges as she'd tumbled backward out of an airplane and let the altimeter needles spin until the last possible moment, when she'd yanked the parachute cord and flown free. Adrenaline had pushed aside her mother's absence or her father's lack of compromise when she'd leaped from a dozen bridges and train trestles, and waited for the bungee cord to take up the slack of freefall.

Those had been her outlets, the only things that could quiet her soul when it seemed that nothing else was going right in her life.

And now?

Now, she realized with sudden clarity, she needed the exact same thing. A moment of privacy. Of clarity.

Of intentional danger.

She nodded at Max and grinned, though part of

her felt a little mean when she said, "You're right. I'm going climbing."

She'd found the one place Erik Falco couldn't follow, and she was damn well going to take advantage of it.

AN HOUR LATER Erik leaned up against a padded wall and scowled, hoping the frown would discourage idle conversation. But he soon realized he didn't need to bother—the others weren't at the converted warehouse to talk.

They were there to climb.

On either side of him, the walls rose up and curled over to create impossible-seeming angles and overhangs, all formed out of foam and molded fiberglass in colors unimagined by nature. The vertical—and sometimes horizontal—planes were rusty-brown, criss-crossed with wild streaks of turquoise, green and yellow. Deep grooves scored the surfaces, ranging from penpoint-wide to forearm-deep, and improbable blobs of yellow, pink and blue handholds were scattered with apparent random disregard— thickly distributed in some places, thinly scattered in others.

It might have looked like a normal room distorted by a funhouse mirror, if it hadn't been for the climbers.

They were everywhere, wearing a dizzying array of colors and meshwork harnesses, clinging to the walls like fluorescent human spiders caught in webs of thick nylon ropes and metal clips. They worked in teams, one above the other on the wall, or one on the wall, the other standing on the ground manning a long safety rope.

The floors were heavily padded and the air smelled of sweat and healthy fear, with an overtone of talc. It didn't look like any gym Erik had ever frequented, but the grunts of exertion and rumbles of encouragement he heard over the heavy thump of rock music reminded him of being fit. Being active.

Being strong.

"Hey," Meg's voice said at his elbow. Her tone was neutral, but when he turned, he saw questions in her eyes. Then he glanced down at the rest of her and his brain vapor-locked.

The photos his investigators had gathered had included some from charity functions, showing her dressed-to-impress in floor-length gowns or one memorable little black dress. Those photographs had left him with the impression of an elegant woman in her midthirties, self-possessed and confident, tall and solidly built in clothing that never quite showcased the promise he sensed in the body beneath. Since meeting her in person, he'd seen her in work clothes and her lab coat, and even though they'd found themselves at odds over the NPT acquisition, he hadn't been able to shake the sense that she had a better body than she let on.

Now, seeing her ready to do battle with a foam wall, all he could think was damn, he'd been right.

And then some.

She wore tight gym shorts that ended just above

her knees, surprising him with the long length of smooth calf below. He'd known she was tall, but hadn't realized that most of it was leg. Perfect, whole, unmarred leg.

At the thought, he felt a stir of lust coupled with a scrape of resentment.

Her bare feet were encased in thin climbing shoes that flexed as she shifted her weight from one foot to the other. She wore a faded nylon utility belt around her hips, and a hot pink sports bra with a cropped T-shirt overtop. The shirt looked as though she'd gone after it with scissors and cut away the neck, arms and bottom half. It showed as much as it covered, to the point that he wondered why she'd bothered.

Modesty, or something else?

She jerked her head to an opening beyond the colorful walls. "I'll be in the next room. You can stay here if you want. I promise not to sneak out and sabotage my own research." The last was said with a bite of sarcasm.

Partly because he felt like an idiot leaning on the wall by himself, partly because a masochistic section of his brain wanted to watch, Erik grabbed his cane and stepped forward with the same damned awkward lurch he always needed to get moving. "I'm right behind you. I can hold up a wall in there just as easily as I can here."

Her lips tightened, but she turned away. "Come on, then."

Her quick, long-legged strides quickly outpaced

his gimp, which was slowed by the muscle strains of the past few days. Maybe she was trying to lose him. Maybe she was trying to make the point she'd already made too well. Either way, the message was clear.

You don't belong here. I don't want you here.

They both knew damn well that was why she'd come. She didn't want to climb. She wanted to teach him a lesson.

Knowing it, he gritted his teeth and followed her through a sloping archway into the next room, which not only had climbing surfaces on the walls, but also contained a huge geometric figure in the center of the wide space. The rust-colored megalith looked like a UFO, or maybe an abstract artist's impression of a UFO. Made of the same material as the walls, the thing bulged on one side and rose to a high spire on the other. As in the other room, the surface was broken by craggy fissures and brightly colored hand-holds. Similarly, the edifice was dotted here and there by climbers.

Only these climbers were unsupported by ropes.

Erik shot a look at her belt, only then realizing it supported only a bag of chalk and—incongruously—a toothbrush. "You free-sclimb?"

She shot him an indecipherable look. "It's called bouldering. And, yeah. You got a problem with that?" The jut of her chin dared him to say yes, to argue that free-climbing—bouldering, whatever she called it— was a senseless, stupid risk.

But because he didn't have the right, and because

his objections came from another, more complicated source, he shook his head. "No objection. I'll watch from down here. Just don't fall and go splat."

She sniffed. "What? And make your life easier? I don't think so." She turned away, but then paused and glanced back. "Look, would you do me a favor?"

His instincts quivered to life. "What sort of favor?"

She shifted her weight on the balls of her feet, making him elementally aware of the slide of the long, lean muscles in her legs and the unexpectedly defined muscles of her arms. He felt a rush of heat, and shifted on his own feet, feeling the brace of the cane beside him.

"Would you mind waiting in the other room?" she asked. "I know I said you could watch in here, but I could really use the space right now."

He snorted. "What space? We're inside a converted warehouse with a hundred other people. It's not like you're out on Mt. Washington, just you against the elements." Though suddenly he could picture her clinging to a precarious knife-edge ridge of rock in a sharp opposition to the image she projected.

She presented herself as professional. Detached. Untouchable.

All of it was a lie, disguising the woman underneath.

She was none of those things as she glared at him. "It's not my first choice, but it's a good option for blowing off some steam when I don't have time to get out of the city. And, yeah, there are a bunch of people around, but none of them bother me nearly as much as you do. Since you can't spot me—" she looked pointedly at the cane "—I'd rather you left me alone for a bit."

Ouch. Erik buried the wince, knowing she was getting him back for single-handedly putting a stranglehold on her licensing plans.

He could almost see it in her eyes. *You hit me where it hurts and I hit back. How does it feel?*

Not good, but he wasn't going to tell her that. Instead he nodded shortly. "I have your word that you won't leave without me?"

"I promise." But she looked away as she said it, sending his instincts spiking into the danger zone. "I'll climb for an hour, maybe less."

She strode away, comfortable in her thin, flexible shoes with their grippy bottoms. She crossed to the fiberglass UFO, where she met up with a buff, tanned guy probably a few years younger than she. He wore an employee's polo shirt that was cut off at the throat and arms much like her T-shirt and ragged jeans shorts that bared his bronzed, muscled legs.

Erik disliked him on sight, and disliked him even more when he leaned close and said something to Meg, something that sent her burbling laugh rising up and over the background noise of music and exertion. Then she glanced over at Erik and her laugh cut off, as if someone had thrown a switch.

She pantomimed a shooing motion.

He muttered a curse and turned away. She wanted

space? He'd give her space, damn it, but he wasn't trusting her for one moment, promise or not. He limped through the faux rock archway toward the rope climbers, but then turned back and propped his shoulder against the doorway. He could watch from there without being seen, giving her space while also providing protection.

Protection for her from the danger that seemed to be stalking them. Protection for him from being betrayed by an attractive woman. Again.

He muttered a curse as he watched her chalk her hands from the pouch at her waist and attack the free-climbing wall while the stranger spotted her from ground level. It wasn't until a spear of pain lanced through his temples that he realized he was gritting his teeth hard enough to make his molars creak.

The sound was overridden by a stranger's voice at his elbow. "You climbing or just watching?"

Erik turned, annoyed that he'd been caught staring. "Just waiting for a friend."

The stranger was in his midforties and wore the silver hair and tanned, wrinkled skin of an outdoorsman with pride. Unlike most of the other climbers, his shirt was uncut and tucked into loose drawstring pants. Something sparked in the depths of his brown eyes when he held out a hand. "I'm Luke Cannon."

Erik shook because it would have been rude not to, but he could think of only two reasons why the stranger had come over. "If this is a pickup, I'm not interested, and if you're looking for money, I'm not giving."

Cannon snorted. "Don't flatter yourself. I don't swing that way, and I don't need your money. Otto asked me to come over. Meg's friends are his friends, if you get my meaning."

Erik scowled harder. "And Otto would be…?"

The older man jerked his head toward the chiseled male-model type spotting Meg. "He owns the place."

"Which still doesn't explain why you're talking to me. I'm not much for idle conversation."

"I hadn't noticed." Cannon's lips twitched. "I came over to see if you wanted to have a go." He gestured to the roped climbers. "It's not as good as outside, but it's better than sitting at a desk."

Erik turned his back on the climbing wall and the faint surge of wistfulness, and focused his attention into the other room, where Meg was halfway up the UFO. As he watched, she swung from her fingertips in an arc that brought her to a bright yellow handhold and a new point of purchase. He grimaced. "Not interested. Like I said, I'm just waiting for a friend."

And even that was an overstatement. He and Meg were hardly friends.

"Fair enough." There was a rustle of cloth as Cannon dug into the back pocket of his warm-up pants and withdrew a nylon wallet. He pulled out a business card. "This is neither a come-on or a request for money, but if you ever change your mind, give me a call."

"I won't." But Erik took the card and glanced at it as Cannon walked away with an awkward, rolling gait. The simple cream-colored stock was embossed "Luke Cannon, Pentium Pharmaceuticals."

Pharma, eh? It might have been a simple coincidence. The gym was located in the center of the hospital district. It was a good bet that more than half of the climbers were hospital or research types.

But that didn't explain why Cannon had come over to him.

Erik tucked the card into the back pocket of his slacks and turned toward the rope wall just in time to see Cannon strip off his warm-up pants. Metal glinted where Cannon's right leg should have been, and suddenly his overture and the rolling gait made too much sense.

He was an amputee.

A hard, hurting fist clutched in Erik's gut, bringing with it the smell of antiseptic and the fear he'd felt in the hospital as he'd lain there, powerless to do anything but let the IV seep into his veins, one drop at a time, keeping him alive whether he liked it or not.

We may have to take the leg, they'd told his boss, thinking him unconscious when really he lacked the strength to open his eyes and respond. *It might be the best thing for him.*

In the end they hadn't, taking only the dying muscle, the pieces that wouldn't reattach no matter how hard the arthroscopic surgeons worked. They had patched him up and taught him how to walk again, all the while reminding him how lucky he'd been to keep the leg.

But now, as he watched Cannon strap into the climbing gear and begin his ascent, hopping nimbly from one purchase to the next, deftly inserting a specially designed artificial foot into cracks too small to admit flesh and blood, Erik cursed himself for being weak, for being too broken to heal.

Why else did the one-legged man seem like less of a cripple than he did?

He turned away, hating the smell of sweat and activity, which served only to drive home the point that he didn't belong here, didn't belong anywhere.

With a half-formed plan of grabbing Meg and hustling her out on some pretext or another, he stepped into the bouldering room. Two things happened simultaneously.

His cell phone rang.

And he saw that Meg was gone.

Chapter Six

Meg had just negotiated a tricky part of the course Otto had set up for her, one that sent her around the backside of the wall, when she heard Erik bellow, *"Megan!"*

She didn't stop to question how she immediately knew it was him amid the dozen or so other men in the climbing area that knew her name. She didn't want to consider how quickly the timbre of his voice had engraved itself on her consciousness, for good or ill. Instead, she fixed on the fear in his tone.

Something had happened. Something bad.

She quick-timed it back along her route, traversing a narrow crevice that barely held the tips of her climbing mocs, and then swinging around the corner almost blind, her entire weight suspended by the fingertips of her left hand as her right reached for the faraway hold. At deadpoint, the moment when her body stopped swinging up and gravity took over, she stretched extra hard and felt the grippy, sponge-like material beneath her fingertips. She grabbed it, felt sinew and muscle stretch, and then released with her left hand, letting gravity turn her into a pendulum as she lifted her legs and aimed for a narrow ledge that was maybe three inches wide.

For a moment she was weightless. Flying. Free. Nothing else mattered. Then her toes hooked the ledge and she balanced there, no longer weightless, now shackled to the wall by the bonds of gravity and shackled to the present by the glowering man who stood twenty feet below.

She turned and leaned back against the wall with her heels braced on the ledge, resentful that he'd interrupted and annoyed that she felt a sharp slice of guilt. She'd brought him here not just because she'd needed the release of physical activity, but because she'd needed to prove something to herself by seeing him here.

She'd wanted to remind herself that he wasn't for her. Not on a professional level, and not on a physical level. She was trying to rediscover her exciting, physical side. He'd lost his along the way, and was too busy being mad at the world to try to find a new path.

The knowledge sharpened her voice when she said, "Yell a little louder, why don't you? I'm not sure the beginner's belay class heard you out in the front room."

He exhaled through his nose, displeasure crackling in the air between them. She was aware that a few of the climbers sharing the central boulder with her were tuned in to the conversation, while others concentrated on their climbing, minding their own business. "Come down here," Erik said, his tone quieter but no less sharp. "Please."

She bent her knees and eased down from the ledge, catching a series of handholds and footholds on the way down. If she'd been outside on an unfamiliar wall with only a small, portable pad below her, she would've taken it slower. As it was, the floor was heavily padded and she was familiar with the indoor line. She descended effortlessly. Fluidly.

Freely.

She was breathing hard when she touched down, feeling the ache of exertion, the steady thud of her heart, which reminded her how good it was to be fit again, to be active again. How important activity was to her.

And how much it would hurt to lose.

The padding gave beneath her as she turned and strode toward Erik.

"You bellowed?" She shot a hip and moved to stick her hands in her pockets, but they glanced off the smoothness of her climbing shorts. She crossed her arms, hoping she looked tough rather than defensive. "Look, about Luke Cannon. I don't want you to think—"

He reached out and gripped her forearms, pulling her arms straight, forcing her guard down as he looked at her, blue eyes intent on her face. "I didn't see you. I thought you'd disappeared on me."

The raggedness in his voice had her biting back her first retort. Instead she turned her arms beneath his hands, so his fingers slid down and, almost unconsciously, linked with hers.

Still aware of the curiosity of the other climbers, the weight of Otto's stare from the shadows, she thought about pulling away, but didn't. She couldn't have said why. Instead she tightened her fingers on his. "I was just on the other side of the boulder. I'm okay."

But she saw from his eyes that it wasn't just that she'd been out of his line of sight. Something else had happened.

"What is it?" she asked, suddenly dreading the answer.

His voice went hollow when he said, "It's Raine. She's just been rushed to the ER. It looks like a stroke."

ERIK USED HIS SHOULDER to shove through the ER doors and almost fell inside when they gave. He was aware of the curious stares from the other occupants of the waiting room when he stumped across the room at top speed. At his side, Meg strode grim-faced. She'd spent the short taxi ride on the phone, trying to reach her lab or one of the doctors on the case. But the lab was six-o'clock empty and the ER nurses were trained to fend off inquiries.

Immediate family only, they'd said, and when she pressed doctor-to-nurse she'd gotten, *We don't know anything yet.*

When they arrived at the main desk, Meg had her hospital ID at the ready. "Raine Montgomery," she snapped. "Which room?"

The lady behind the desk raised an eyebrow. "Excuse me, *Doctor?*"

Erik didn't quite understand the sneer in her voice, but he'd been around enough deals-gone-bad to know where this one was headed. He nudged Meg out of the way—perhaps more forcefully than necessary—and slapped a warm, concerned expression on his face. "Forgive my friend. She's worried. We both are. Raine is important to us."

It wasn't until he'd said the words that he realized they were true. Not in the way he suspected Raine wanted, but he'd come to trust her. He, who didn't trust pretty women, trusted Raine. She was important to him.

Yeah, an internal voice sneered, *so important that you've left her on her own while you chase a woman just like Celia.*

The nurse's expression softened a hint, but she said, "I really can't give out information to nonfamily members."

"I'm her boss, and I know the doc here comes on strong, but she means well. Cut us a break." Erik lowered his voice. "Raine is divorced, she's lost contact with her foster parents and I work her so hard she doesn't have time for a social life. I count as her family."

The nurse's lips twitched almost involuntarily. "If she's lost contact with her family, then who's the 'brother' in there waiting on her? Big guy named Max."

"Another friend," Erik answered as he wondered why Meg's second-in-command was taking a personal interest. He leaned closer and lowered his voice. "What do you say? Can you help us out here?"

The nurse's eyes cut from him to Meg and back before her chin dipped. "Okay. You can go on through. Third floor, Surgery Suite 3B."

Erik gave the woman his best grin, then had to hurry to catch Meg. They rode the elevator in a silence broken only by a beep from his pocket, indicating that his data unit had received a text message.

"Turn that thing off," Meg snapped. "You're in a hospital."

"Right. Sorry." He hit the kill switch on the transmitter, turning the pocket-size unit into a nontransmitting PDA. When he clicked over to view the text message, he got nothing. He cursed and reminded himself to buy a new one ASAP. This was the second time in the past few days it had glitched out on him. "Stupid piece of garbage."

Then the elevator doors opened and he saw Max sitting in a small, austerely furnished waiting area.

Meg crossed to him. "What's the situation?"

They conferred briefly in med-speak that Erik interpreted by the expression on Meg's face, which went from grave to graver, though she kept a professional front when she turned to him. "Raine's in surgery. She developed a clot in her right lung, and may have suffered a small stroke."

Though that had been the gist of Max's initial phone call, it still didn't make sense. "I thought she was being treated."

"We were too late." But the wrinkle in Meg's

brow suggested it was more than that. She glanced at Max. "Maybe she'd formed some clots in larger, more resistant vessels and the IF-G treatment broke them apart and moved them."

"Or?" Erik prompted, hearing the qualifier in her voice.

"Or maybe there's something else going on. A trigger. A problem with the baby, perhaps, or an outside agent."

"Preeclampsia?" Max said. He hadn't moved from his seated position except to toss a magazine on a low table in the center of the room. His body was etched with fatigue and frustration. Professional or personal? Erik wasn't sure.

Worse, he didn't think he had the right to ask.

"It's possible," Meg agreed. "But what triggered the problem? Our treatment? Or something else?"

A door at the far end of the waiting area swung inward to reveal a gowned figure.

"How is she?" Erik demanded.

The surgeon, whose nametag said Oberman, looked past him and latched on to Meg. "Dr. Corning, can I have a word with you in private?"

"No," Erik said flatly. "Say what you need to out here. If a mistake's been made, I want to know about it right now."

At Oberman's inquiring glance, Meg nodded. "Go ahead."

"If you insist," the surgeon said, doubt evident in his voice. "I'll start by saying she has a very good chance of pulling through. We got the pulmonary embolism, and her vitals are rebounding nicely. They're finishing up now, and from there she'll go to recovery. You should be able to visit her within the hour."

"And the baby?" Max asked quickly.

"Fine for now, but she's probably looking at bed rest for the duration."

Erik winced, knowing Raine would hate the confinement.

"What else?" Meg asked, voice tight.

"You'd just started her on interferon treatment, right?"

She nodded. "Today was day four. She seemed to be tolerating it well. We did blood work before and after, and—"

The surgeon shifted his weight on his feet as though tired, or maybe uncomfortable with asking, "You're sure it was interferon?"

"Of course." Meg furrowed her brows. "Why?"

"Because her clotting factor was off the charts. When we looked at it more carefully, she tested positive for Clotting Factor VII. Her levels were three times the therapeutic dose." The surgeon focused on Meg. "Any idea how she might've gotten something like that in her system?"

Fury tightened Erik's gut and he spun on her.

Suddenly he didn't see a statuesque red-blonde in front of him. He saw a bleached-blonde, all bones and angles and cool, knowing eyes. "What are you playing at? Did you think I'd back off the deal if she was sick?" The color blanched from Meg's face.

Erik leveled a finger at her. "I trusted you with her! I trusted—"

"Enough!" Meg put both hands on his chest and shoved, sending him back two staggering paces and nearly putting him on his ass. "You're beyond out of line. I gave her the proper treatment, and to hell with you if you don't believe me."

Erik growled and reached for her as Oberman grabbed a wall phone and said sternly, "You've got thirty seconds to chill, pal, or I'm calling security."

As if on cue, the phone beeped. Only it wasn't the phone, Erik realized moments later. It was his PDA.

The waiting text message.

It was probably nothing, he told himself. The important stuff was going on in this room, where Meg's ghost-pale face now had two dots of temper riding high across her cheekbones. But something had him reaching for his pocket and pulling out the PDA.

Text Message Received.

"No kidding. You received it ten minutes ago, you piece of—" He broke off and pulled up the message.

The screen showed three simple, terrifying lines that put things on a whole new level.

Received from: Unknown
Message: Kill the deal.
Next time it'll be your other girlfriend.

Chapter Seven

Dr. Oberman cleared Raine to have visitors a short time later. After trying several times to contact the detectives, Erik headed to her room.

She wasn't alone.

Max sat in the visitor's chair. As Erik watched, the big man touched Raine's hand.

She stirred and blinked, then closed her eyes again and sighed. "Hey, boss. I'm glad you came. I have something to say to you."

A dark look crossed Max's face. "I'm not—"

Erik stepped into the room. "I'm here, Raine."

She smiled faintly, eyes still closed. "Thinking you're going to die does interesting things to your priorities. I wanted you to know that I'm sorry I've been weird with you lately. I got it in my head that I was in love with you, that we could go from pretending to be a family to actually being one." She tried to laugh, but it trailed off into a sigh. "I just wanted you to know that it's okay. You don't have to worry about me—I'll be fine by myself. I always am."

Erik stood frozen in the hospital room doorway, feeling like the biggest jerk to ever walk the face of the earth as a single tear traced its way down Raine's sallow cheek.

He hadn't handled her crush well at all. They were adults. They should have sat down and talked it out like adults. Instead he'd let it go on too long and he'd hurt someone he trusted. Someone he relied on.

Someone he…well, loved was too strong a word for him, but someone who had become important to him over the years.

Someone he hadn't meant to hurt.

Raine's breathing evened into that of sleep. Max stood up from the bedside chair, his expression dark. "I should go."

Erik shifted on his feet, or rather on his cane, which he had a sudden mad urge to hurl through the window. He didn't want to talk about what had just happened—not with Meg's employee, not with anyone.

Knowing it made him look like a bastard and not entirely sure he didn't deserve the label, he focused on the case, saying, "Now that Meg's not in the room, you have any idea how Raine got the clotting factor in her?"

Max regarded him levelly. "As I'm sure Meg already told you, we gave her the prescribed treatment, nothing more." He glanced back at the bed, where Raine's face had gained a faint blush, as though her subconscious mind already regretted the truths she'd confessed. The he turned back to Erik and his expression hardened. "And as I'm sure you already know, Raine deserves better. She and Meg both do."

He stalked toward the door, bumping Erik hard enough to knock him back a step. Then he was gone, leaving Erik alone with a sleeping Raine.

Kill the deal. The words spooled through his mind. *Next time it'll be your other girlfriend.*

Raine. Meg. Neither was his girlfriend, but both had been endangered because of him. Because of "the deal," which could only refer to the NPT technology.

But he couldn't kill the deal. He needed the technology, needed the facet that Meg was so determined to block from being developed. It might be his last chance to ever walk normally again, to ever be a whole man again. His life, his career had been focused on nothing else for the past five years. This was it, he could feel it. He was sure of it.

But what if the cost was too great?

"I don't know." He said the words out loud, feeling them echo deep within his soul. What was wholeness worth to him?

He crossed the room and sank into the chair beside Raine. He didn't take her hand because he didn't deserve to touch her. Hell, he didn't deserve to sit beside her. She was a beautiful, wonderful, passionate woman, and she had wanted him.

How had he returned the favor? He'd put her in the path of a killer. And now he couldn't bring himself to back down, even if it meant endangering the life of another woman, one whose motives were far less pure but who didn't deserve the danger any more than Raine did.

He cursed and dropped head to his hands, filled with the knowledge that he was quite possibly the most selfish man in the universe.

Detective Peters's voice spoke from the doorway. "Falco? You called?" The two detectives stood outside in the hallway.

Erik levered himself to his feet and nodded to the door. "Let's find somewhere we can talk. I've got our answer."

Peters glanced from the bed to Erik and back. "To which question?"

"I'm the target. Or rather, my acquisition of Meg's technology is the target."

He handed his PDA to Detective Sturgeon, who frowned as he read the text message. "Let's find Dr. Corning," the detective said after a moment's silence. "She'll need to be in on this conversation."

"I'd rather—" Erik caught himself, knowing it wasn't about what he'd rather do. Not anymore. "You're right. I'll find her and bring her in on the meeting."

And he'd make a few phone calls while he was at it, see if he could move up the timetable to day five rather than seven. Once the deal was done, there would be no more reason for his enemy—whoever the hell it was—to threaten the women. Meg would hate him for it, but he told himself the end justified the means.

It was for her own good.

ERIK WAS UP TO SOMETHING. Meg could feel it in the tense air of the conference room across the hall from her lab, where they were meeting with the detectives in what had become a council of war.

"I think we're looking at this the wrong way," she said into a small pause in the flow of masculine conversation. When the men looked at her, she placed her hands flat on the cool surface of the table, trying to project calm competence in the face of a situation she wasn't fully equipped to handle.

Skydiving and snowboarding uncharted runs were one thing. Being targeted by someone who wanted to kill her was another.

"How do you suggest we look at it?" Erik asked, not meeting her eyes.

"You're focusing on your personal enemies, people who wouldn't want you to have a major financial success from developing the NPT technology." She swallowed, surprising herself with the realization that she didn't hate the idea of the sale as much as she had a few days earlier.

The more she'd gotten to know Erik, the more she'd started to, if not like him, at least respect his integrity.

Baloney. You're making excuses because you're attracted to him.

She felt her face heat as she said, "I think we need to figure out who might want the technology completely blocked. That would explain why the accidents with the cement and the elevator looked like they were aimed at me."

Detective Peters nodded. "True, but you gave us

a list after the first incident. We haven't had a connection pop yet."

"And besides," Erik said, voice rough, "Raine's attack was clearly aimed at me."

"Yes and no," Meg said, not even sure why she was arguing. Her gut knotted with the theories and suspicions they'd been discussing for a solid half hour, and her pounding headache reminded her that it was nearly midnight, that she hadn't slept well the night before, alone in her place, only partially soothed by the regular police patrols. "Raine's collapse threw suspicion on my lab. If it hadn't been for the text message, you'd probably still think we messed up and gave her the clotting meds." When he didn't deny the fact, she sighed on a faint wash of disappointment.

It wasn't until that moment that she realized she'd been fishing for something more from him. That was just stupid. And irrational. And pointless.

She dug her nails into her palms, the pain reminding her to stay on point when her libido wanted to wander into asinine, dangerous territory. Just because she'd lost weight and started climbing again didn't make her the type to leap without a parachute.

Especially when she was pretty sure there wouldn't be anyone waiting to catch her.

"So what are you suggesting?" Erik said, still not making eye contact, which made her wonder just what he was hiding this time. He continued, "Somehow I doubt you're planning on pulling NPT from the playing field. It's out there. You can't take it back unless you want to claim that it's having problems in testing." He shot her a look. "*Is* it having problems?"

"Of course not," she snapped. "NPT works. It's a breakthrough. A potential blockbuster that'll redefine the industry. That's why they—whoever they are—want it stopped." She paused and took a breath. "I'm proposing that we let the licensing deal go through. I have one last company interested in the NPT with my restrictions. I'm saying we do that deal and see what happens."

She expected an explosion from Erik. Instead his voice went deadly flat. "Not an option."

"It'll separate out the threads," she argued, focusing her plea on the detectives. "If the threat is directed at FalcoTechno, then nothing happens, or the danger focuses on Erik and his next deal. If the threat is aimed at me, at getting NPT off the market…" She trailed off, unwilling to voice the possibilities.

"Then you're bait." Erik surged to his feet and began to pace, barely leaning on his cane. "He'll be coming straight after you."

"Which is no different from the situation right now," she countered, trying to sound calm when her stomach and head were in competition with each other in the discomfort Olympics.

He glared. "You're using this situation to your advantage, to push through a license the administration normally wouldn't agree to, just so you don't have to sell to me."

"Yes, I am." She stood and faced him, aware of Sturgeon taking notes, of Peters watching them with hooded, considering eyes. "And you'd do the same thing if you were in my position. You're just mad because you didn't get it done first."

They faced off opposite each other for a long, tense moment before he sighed and looked away. "Don't do something you'll regret later, Meg."

Meg. Once again, his use of her first name did something strange to her insides, something that shouldn't be associated with a man such as him, one who blocked her at every turn, who matched her on a mental level but lagged behind physically.

Or so she kept telling herself.

"Enough." Sturgeon climbed to his feet. "We're not getting anywhere here, and we're not using you as bait for anything until we have a better idea of what's going on."

"He's right," Peters said, gathering his electronic notepad along with Erik's PDA. "It's late and it's been a long few days. Let's get some rest and come back at this tomorrow." He glanced from Erik to Meg and back again. "You two watch your backs."

"Of course." Erik turned so he was shoulder-to-shoulder with her, so they were suddenly united rather than opposed. "I'll stay with her. Wouldn't mind if you had a car cruise past her place every half hour or so, too."

Sturgeon nodded. "You got it."

While the men arranged to meet again midmorning, Meg fumed. When the detectives were gone, she turned on Erik. "'I'll stay with her?' What kind of macho bull is that? Who asked you to stay?"

She was aware of her volume climbing, aware that she shouldn't be arguing when she didn't want to head home to her empty place alone. Not again. But stress and fear and a shivery ball of energy in her gut combined to make her prickly and reactive. Over-reactive maybe, but damn it, didn't she have the right to a tantrum at this point?

"Do you honestly want to stay by yourself?" He arched a dark eyebrow and she damned him for saying what she'd just thought.

"I assumed you'd want to stay with Raine," she said, aiming where it would hurt both of them. When his eyes darkened, she retreated a step. "I mean… I thought… Oh, hell. I don't know."

Darkness flickered briefly in his eyes. "Yeah, I know what you mean." He advanced a step, until they were closer than they'd been when they were fighting, closer than they should be now.

Meg was acutely aware of the silence of the building around them. It was well past quitting time, and the quiet of desertion was punctuated by the occasional click and hum of expensive machinery. The janitors had come and gone. The floor was locked and key-coded.

They were completely, utterly alone.

She was conscious of the quick rise and fall of Erik's broad chest as their spat of moments ago morphed into something hotter and more dangerous.

"This is stupid," she said, as much to herself as to him. "I don't like you. I don't trust you. I shouldn't be attracted to you."

"Same goes," he said, a flash of something like amusement, something like anger, crossing his face. "Then again, that seems to be my usual M.O. What's your excuse?"

But even though his words came out faintly mocking, he closed the distance between them, until she could feel the warmth of him against the suddenly sensitized skin of her cheeks and lips. "Stupidity, maybe. The situation. The circumstances. Hell, even the danger, I don't know."

But she did. That last choice resonated a little too well, but the moment was lost when he closed the gap between them. Their lips touched. Their breaths mingled.

And their last shreds of rationality were lost.

Chapter Eight

Meg was free-falling without a parachute. The rushing in her ears was the sound of the wind, the pounding of her heart was the feel of danger. Adrenaline. Exhilaration.

Except she had solid ground beneath her feet. It wasn't the wind at all. It was Erik.

His lips cruised against hers, the rasp of late-night stubble on his cheeks and chin adding a rough edge to the softness, a thrill to the demand. Then she was the one demanding, parting her lips beneath his and diving headfirst into the heat.

The temptation.

She fisted her hands in his shirt and pulled him close even as a faint buzz in the back of her brain warned that this wasn't one of the smartest moves she'd ever made.

But of the dumb decisions she'd ever made, this was the one that felt the best.

She sank into the kiss, into the man, sliding her fingers from his shirt to his shoulders, then his arms.

She felt strong, corded muscles beneath her fingers, and was faintly surprised at their leashed power. She raked her fingernails across his biceps and felt him shudder.

Then he gripped her hips in his big hands, so his thumbs rested low on her pelvis, and it was her turn to shudder. Neurons she'd all but forgotten about flared to life, reminding her of the woman she'd been before her job responsibilities and her father's pressure to "tone it down" had turned her into someone else.

Someone she was bound and determined to outgrow, damn it. Starting now, with this surprising man who was nothing like what she'd thought she wanted, but had somehow become exactly what she needed.

She angled her head to accept more of his mouth, demand more of it, and he complied, delving deep with his tongue and gripping her hips so hard she thought he would leave marks. She moaned her pleasure, and when he stiffened and hesitated, she whispered, "More. Please, more."

He froze and ended the kiss. Dropped his arms from around her. Backed up a step.

And looked down at her, breathing hard.

Suddenly ashamed for no reasons she could pinpoint besides the quick chill of his eyes and the rapid beat of blood beneath her skin, she crossed her arms over her chest to form a pitiful barrier, acutely aware of the rasp of material across her tender nipples. She swallowed hard and fought for humor when she couldn't read his expression. "I don't suppose you'd care to drop the purchase offer, huh?"

His eyes blanked in an instant. "Is that what you want?"

She'd meant it as a joke, but as passion drained, all of the complications rushed in, reminding her that this wasn't about the man-woman stuff, had never been about that.

It was about NPT. About someone wanting it, or not wanting him to have it. If he backed out, maybe things would settle down. Maybe the danger would pass.

Maybe nobody else would get hurt.

So she nodded. "That's what I've always wanted." A small internal voice reminded her that a few moments earlier, her wants had had very little to do with molecular biology and everything to do with chemistry. Man-woman chemistry. Erik and Meg chemistry.

His voice slapped like an accusation when he said, "Is that why you kissed me?"

She fell back, confused. Anger flared on the heels of that confusion. "You kissed me first. What's your excuse?"

"I'm an idiot." He jammed one hand in his pocket and gripped his cane with the other as he paced away, then back, his uneven stride growing jerkier by the moment. "I—"

He cut off the word with a click of teeth and blanked his expression to the point that he barely looked human anymore. He could've been a statue.

The thought of him bunking on her couch, or worse, in an adjoining hotel room, lent a new frisson of energy to the worry. "I'm not sure I want you as my protection."

He scowled and advanced on her until they were nearly nose-to-nose, until he filled her vision, looking large and angry and masculine, capable of protection, of violence, every inch the cop he'd once been. "Sorry, babe. You don't have a choice. I'm the one with the gun."

Though she knew he wasn't threatening her, she fell back a step and bumped into the conference table. "I thought you said you didn't carry anymore, that the recoil messed with your balance."

"I said I didn't like to carry," he corrected her. "I never said I couldn't. I can and will if the circumstances require, and these do. So I'll ask again, your place or a hotel?"

"My place," she said finally, because the narrow house had three different floors. She could get away from him if she needed to, away from his presence and the memory of that chilly transformation, when he'd gone from aroused to stone-cold in an instant.

He tipped his head in assent and gestured toward the elevators. "You go. I'll cover you."

And he did just that as they left the building, eyes probing every niche, every shadow. Oddly, instead of making her feel safer, his vigilance made her feel more endangered.

More exposed.

EDWARD WATCHED from his vantage point at a small pastry shop down the street from Boston General. Open late, the six-table restaurant had allowed him to watch in comfort, with the added benefits of strong coffee and delicacies he'd paid for singly, much to the waitress's amusement.

Let her laugh. The moment Falco and the doctor emerged, Edward tossed his napkin, drained his espresso and dropped a decent tip on the table before he strode out into the night and hailed a cab.

"Where to?" the driver asked once the door was shut, closing Edward in with the scents of cheap plastic and too many other people.

"Wait one moment."

That earned him a startled look, but the cabbie shrugged. "Meter's running."

Edward watched as Falco's Mercedes emerged from the Boston General underground lot. "Follow that car."

"You some sort of a stalker or something?" But the cabbie said it with a laugh.

Edward snorted. "Hardly. We've been at an office party. The boss asked me to make sure they get home okay, but not to make a big deal about it, if you know what I mean."

The driver glanced in the rearview mirror, making Edward worry that the lie was too elaborate. Then the cabbie's eyes slid away and he steered them out into the sparse midnight traffic on Kneeland Street. "Bummer. I was hoping for something more exciting."

"Sorry to disappoint."

They tailed the Mercedes to a row of neat, narrow houses just outside überexpensive Beacon Hill. "Don't pull up too close when they get out," Edward warned. "The boss didn't want his top VP to know I was checking up."

"Gotcha." The driver rolled to a stop in the lee of a big green van, so they were partially blocked from view as Falco and the bitch emerged and walked up a brick path toward her house. They walked near each other but not together, separated by a telling empty space, and by their stiff, stilted postures. The cabbie noticed it, too. "Looks like they had a fight in the car. That, or the drink's wearing off."

"Either way, I'm just making sure they get home safe." He watched as the doctor unlocked the front door and Falco shielded her with his body, just like a good little cop. They went in together. The door shut. The lights snapped on inside. Edward leaned back and smiled. "That'll do. You can drop me at the closest T stop."

The driver's reflection in the rearview mirror looked faintly insulted that his fare would rather take public transport the rest of the way home. In reality, Edward planned to switch cabs at the station, then again at least once more before giving his home address. Just in case.

But as the cab rolled back onto the street, those practicalities were lost in a wave of satisfaction.

It wouldn't be long now.

ERIK CHECKED every room in Meg's house, from the lower-level storage and guest room, through the main level with its open kitchen and sitting area, up to the top floor, where he discovered a sybaritic master suite that gave him way too many ideas. The bed was neatly made with a green knitted spread that contrasted with the rich burgundy paint on the walls and the brass accents of the headboard and bedside lamps.

He shouldn't be able to picture Meg lying there, beckoning him closer.

Because he could, because his system still revved from the kiss they'd shared back at the hospital, and from the surge of mindless, near-violent anger that had consumed him when she'd asked him about the NPT deal in the heat of the moment, he realized he'd done it again. He'd fallen in lust with a woman who didn't want him, but rather wanted something *from* him.

"Idiot."

"Did you find something?" Her voice came from the doorway, startling him. Inflaming him.

He spun on her, gun in one hand, cane in the other. "I thought I told you to stay by the door."

"That was nearly ten minutes ago. If there was someone here, you'd've found him by now."

He hated the logic, hated the way she stood framed in the doorway with the soft hallway light spilling over her shoulders, touching her cheek and chin with a reflected rosy hue. Tension snapped in the air between them, a sudden acknowledgment of where they were, an awareness of the big bed a few paces away and the pounding, unfulfilled ache of their earlier kiss.

If he were the man he'd once been, he would have damned the consequences and taken her. He would have crossed the room on strong, whole legs, swept her up into his arms and carried her to the bed. Hell, maybe they wouldn't have even made it to the bed the first time. Maybe he would've taken her up against the wall, pounded himself into her until he could think straight again. Until they both could.

But he wasn't that man anymore. He could no more cross the room unassisted as he could lose himself in a woman he didn't trust. So he slid the safety on his weapon—a small drop piece that was all he could handle these days without fighting the recoil—and stuck it into his waistband at the small of his back, where it made an awkward, half-familiar bulge.

Then he leaned on his cane and crossed the room, expecting her to be smart enough to move before he got too close. She didn't, of course, because her agenda was different from his. She'd followed him upstairs with a plan. A purpose.

She wanted to seduce him out of his goal.

He stopped just shy of where she stood, looking up at him with wide eyes and wide lips that beckoned him with a faint hint of tension. Of moist heat.

Again, he was tempted to take her up on the offer. Tempted to believe he could lose himself in the physical without making the emotional mistake he once had.

He leaned closer, until he could smell the faintest hint of her scent, more organic than the touch of perfume in the master bedroom, somehow changed by a day on her skin.

She didn't lean into him, didn't lean away, not even when he shifted to align their faces, their bodies. They weren't touching, but neither were they separated. The heat in the air bound them together.

Her lips shaped a word. Two syllables. His name. "Erik?"

It was barely a puff of breath. An acknowledgment. An invitation. An almost impossible temptation.

He cursed and pulled away. "I thought so. Excuse me." He pushed past her, leaning harder on his cane than necessary, until the force sang up his shoulder and echoed in his hip as he stalked out into the hall and spun back, nearly vibrating with an emotion he couldn't name. "For the record, I'm interested, but I'm not an idiot. You want me? Then tell Cage to go forward with the sale tomorrow. Once that's out of the way, we can get as horizontal as you want."

Her expression blanked with shock for an instant, then flushed with fury. He half expected her to slap him, half wished she would. Instead she straightened away from the door frame, so the light from the brass bedroom lamps gleamed around her like a halo. "I won't prostitute my work, and I won't prostitute myself. I think it's a shame that you would, Erik. A damned shame."

With that, she disappeared into the bedroom. Her voice carried out into the hall. "Help yourself to whatever's in the fridge. Blankets and pillows are in the hallway closet, the sofa's on the middle floor, guest bed on the lower level. Take your pick. And, Erik?"

"Yeah?" he said, though he almost said, *I'm sorry for being a jerk, sorry I'm damaged, sorry for everything.* But he couldn't say any of those things because they weren't really true. He wasn't sorry. He was smart.

"I don't want to see your face until morning."

THOUGH SHE WAS TREMBLING as much from rage as emotional backlash, Meg held it together until she heard his uneven steps move down the hall. She crossed the room and stayed quiet while the hallway closet door opened, then shut, and the stairs creaked beneath his weight.

Then she yanked a pillow off the bed and hurled it against the door. She would've thrown something more satisfyingly solid, something that would've made a glorious crash, but the noise would only bring him running, and that was the last thing she needed.

Ignoring the part of her that said it was *exactly* what she needed, she stalked into the master bath, shedding her clothes as she went. Her stomach rumbled with hunger, but she'd be damned if she faced him again that night.

Two rejections per day was her limit.

Instead she leaned over the Jacuzzi tub and twisted the knobs. She was tired, achy and sore, and she was going to indulge herself, damn it. She'd learned over the past few years that if she didn't take the time, nobody was going to take it for her.

Tears prickling at the thought, at the accumulated stress of the past week, she added bath beads to the filling tub, which was a deep triangle with power nozzles, big enough for two.

When it was full, she grabbed the cordless handset from the bedroom, returned to the bathroom and climbed into the tub. Warmth surrounded her immediately, caressing her with scented bath oils and the low-grade pulse of the jets.

It was almost, but not quite, like being held.

Her eyelids burned as she hit number six on the speed dial and tried not to notice that four of the top five numbers were local take-out restaurants with free delivery.

The line connected halfway through the third ring. "Hello?"

Meg sighed and eased lower in the tub, keeping her phone barely above the surface. "I've decided to become a lesbian. I'm terrible with men." She paused. "Then again, I'm not so good with women, either, so the lesbian thing might not work. What if I bought a little cabin in the Vermont woods and talked to bears, instead?"

There was a startled pause, then a tentative, "Meg? Is that you? Is something wrong at the lab?"

Embarrassment was a hot rush when she realized

that her closest female friend didn't know her phone voice, couldn't conceive of her calling outside of work. "Yes, it's me. I'm sorry, Jemma. I shouldn't have bothered you at home."

"No, that's…" Rustling carried down the line, and the click of a lamp, then her assistant's voice returned, stronger and more awake now. "No. I'm glad you called. What was that about lesbians?"

"Oh, heck. It's late, isn't it?" Meg glanced around, but even *she* wasn't compulsive enough to have a clock in the bathroom. "I'm sorry. I'll hang up now. Please forget I called."

"No. Don't go," Jemma said quickly. "What's wrong? Has there been another attack? Has Raine taken a downturn? No," she answered her own question, "you called to talk about lesbian bears. You've got man trouble?" She gasped. "You went out with Otto?"

Meg remembered her fledgling crush on her climbing instructor with a faint sense of nostalgia. "Nothing that simple. It's Falco."

There was dead silence for a moment before Jemma said, "What was that you were saying about a cabin in the Vermont woods?"

Ouch. Meg sank lower in the bath and told herself the sudden chill was a sign that the bath water was cooling. "You don't like him."

"It's not that," Jemma said quickly, "I like him fine, except for the parts where he tried to strong-arm the administration into selling your life's work, pretended he and Raine were married, put you in the crosshairs of someone who wants you dead, and still manages to act like it's everyone else's fault."

"I thought you said you liked him fine," Meg said, hating that her voice sounded so small, and hating that every one of Jemma's words resonated with inescapable logic.

"I do. Just not for you." After a pause, Jemma sighed. "I'm sorry, I'm not trying to be mean, but you've been out of the dating scene for a few years, right? Well, let's just say I wouldn't suggest breaking the drought with someone like Falco. He's got too much attitude. Too much baggage. Cut your teeth on someone easier. Please."

There was a sharp thread of emotion in Jemma's voice that told Meg she spoke from experience, but the logic rang true. Erik wasn't easy. He was work.

And he'd already turned her down. Twice.

Meg sighed. "How old are you again? You sound like somebody's mother." Not hers, though. And her father had managed to turn the birds and the bees into a two-month lecture series.

"Sorry." Jemma laughed, but the sound carried a thin quality that made Meg wonder. She hadn't asked her assistant many personal questions. She knew Jemma was divorced and childless, and sometimes dated a radiation safety officer named Chet, but beyond that, nothing. Yet her first instinct had been to call Jemma. What did that mean? That she was so socially cut off that she had to turn an employee into an unwilling friend? Or that she was finally breaking out of the academic mold?

Meg decided she preferred the latter option, but feared it might be too little, too late when it came to her relationship with Erik.

Or lack thereof.

"It's just that I don't get him. His reactions don't make sense. One minute I could swear he's going to kiss me—" *Or he is kissing me,* she thought but didn't say, because she wasn't sure she was ready to share the details "—and the next minute he's angry about it. Or maybe angry at me. I'm not sure anymore."

"That's my point," Jemma said. "He's not a bad guy, but—never mind the fact that he's trying to take over your life's work, which can't be a good start for a relationship—he seems like he's got a bunch of layers, and not all of them are good ones. I'd be afraid that if you dug your way through a few of them, you might not like what you find underneath."

"And that's a good enough reason not to bother trying?" Meg asked, hearing the petulance in her own voice and wondering why she was arguing when she knew Jemma was right.

"Maybe, maybe not. But are you willing to invest the time and energy in a project that might not pay off?"

"What if we called him a side project?" Meg said, referring to the smaller, riskier experiments they occasionally attempted. Side projects weren't the main focus of the lab's efforts and they failed ninety percent of the time. But when they succeeded, the payoff was usually huge.

Hell, the technique that eventually became NPT

had evolved from her grad school side project, and NPT was an unqualified success.

"I've worked for you how long?" Jemma asked. "Three years? I think I know you well enough to say there's no way you could make a man like Falco into a side project. Otto, maybe. But Falco? No way. He'd become your primary investment way too quickly."

"Yet you'd rather see me with Otto than Erik," Meg said, beginning to think she would've been better off calling speed dials one through four and ordering take-out.

"I don't think either of them is right for you, but I'd rather see you *practice* on Otto, yes. Much less potential for bloodshed."

Meg shivered faintly at how true those words had already proven. "You're right. I don't like it, but I know you're right." On the heels of the shiver came an ear-popping yawn that she didn't even bother to cover.

Jemma laughed. "Falling asleep on me? Or are you faking to get out of this conversation?"

"Sorry. Long day. Hell, long year." Meg shifted in the tub, pleasantly surprised to realize the jets had done their work, easing the sore spots and loosening the tight muscles. She yawned again and longed for oblivion, for the opportunity to shut her mind off for a few hours. "I'll let you go. Thanks for talking. And I'm sorry I woke you."

"No. I'm glad you called. Maybe..." Jemma

paused, then said, "Maybe once things are settled with the NPT, we could hang out some time. I'd like to buy you dinner. Maybe pick your brain about grad schools?"

The warmth that spread through Meg at the hesitant question had little to do with the bathwater and everything to do with taking a baby step on the journey from boring scientist to the woman she wanted to be. She smiled. "I'd like that."

"It's a date, then. In a non-lesbian bear sort of way." Jemma was laughing when she hung up.

Meg lay back in the tub a moment longer, feeling relaxed and boneless, and like she'd just run a marathon wearing high heels and a push-up bra. She was tired, but it was a better tired than it had been a half hour earlier.

She had a friend. Or maybe the promise of one. Either way, it was more than she'd started the day with.

She rose from the tub and hit the drain, then indulged herself by crossing the big bathroom and stepping into the shower stall, where she sluiced off the last of the bath oil and scrubbed her hair. It was a waste of water, but if she didn't indulge herself after an awful day, who would?

Erik might, an insidious tendril of thought said, reminding her of the heat in his eyes when he'd stood beside her bed, and again when they'd stood chest-to-chest and she'd been sure he was going to kiss her. Sure she was going to let him.

"Jemma's right," she said out loud. "Bad idea. Too much work. Too much risk for too little reward."

Are you sure about the little reward? a tiny voice whispered. She remembered the kiss in the conference room, and her face flamed hotter than the shower steam as she emerged and toweled off a body that was suddenly tingling with desire.

"I'm sure," she answered her own question. To prove it, she didn't head back down the stairs and scrounge food. Instead, she pulled on the oversize T-shirt and soft gym shorts that formed her sleeping attire, killed the lights and slipped beneath the sheets of the wide, indulgent bed she'd bought a few months earlier, on the theory of "if you buy it, he will come."

At the time, *he* had been nameless and faceless, a mental amalgam of past lovers from her pre-Boston General days, along with Otto and a few choice movie stars.

Now, she closed her eyes and found that sleep wasn't quite as close as she'd thought. Worse, she feared that when her dreams came, they would have a face. And a name. Erik.

She shivered at the thought, and again when she heard a car roll by on the street outside, pause, and then continue on. The sound reminded her too acutely of the attacks, of the danger. She thought briefly about calling the night shift to see how Raine was doing, but knew they would have paged her if there was a problem. Besides, she was in bed. Safe. Protected by a reluctant hero, asleep somewhere downstairs.

She closed her eyes, unwisely comforted by the thought of him sprawled out on the soft, feminine chintz couch she'd bought last month. Imagining Erik lying there, she used the warm wash of safety—and attraction—to guide her into sleep.

WHEN SHE WOKE, she couldn't breathe.

Her lungs seized up, burning without heat.

She tried to suck in a breath, tried to scream for help. Pain slashed through her, folding her double on the bed. Some part of her was aware that it was light outside, that it was morning and she was alone in her bedroom. But the larger part of her begged for air, for life.

Help me! She struggled to cry out, but no sound emerged. Her ribs ached with the effort as her body fought to scream and her lungs remained closed. *Erik, help me!*

He was downstairs. She could get to him. She had to.

Heart pounding in her ears, in her suddenly empty chest, she struggled from the bed and fell, taking one of the brass bedside lamps with her in a crash of metal and broken bulb.

Her eyes misted, though there was no smoke. The room was clear. Then the smell hit her, acrid and burning though she hadn't drawn a breath through her nose. Hadn't drawn a breath at all.

It smelled like bleach, only stronger. More acrid.

Got. To. Get. Down. Stairs.

Her head spun with the lack of oxygen, but she forced herself onto her hands and knees, forced herself across the room. Forced herself to grab the doorknob.

It didn't turn.

Somewhere in her brain she remembered locking it. She needed to turn the dead bolt the previous owners had installed to keep the kids out when mom and dad needed privacy. But her fingers couldn't do the job. Her eyes couldn't see through the mask of tears. She. Couldn't. Do. It.

A roaring, rushing noise crashed over her, deafening her to everything but the jerky beat of her heart. She heard the beat falter. Slow. Stumble. And she knew she was dying.

She slumped against the door, boneless.

The last thing she heard was someone shouting her name.

Chapter Nine

"Meg!" Erik pounded on the locked door and cursed when it held. The crash had woken him and brought him running. The silence on the other side of the door had him near panic. "Meg, damn it, answer me this instant or I'm going to break down the door!"

Nothing.

What could have happened? He was damn sure nobody had gotten past him. Had the bastard come in through the window and taken her?

No. Impossible.

Erik put his face near the door to shout again, but as he drew breath, an invisible fist grabbed his lungs and squeezed. He reeled back, coughing. His nose, eyes and throat burned, and he tasted something foul on the back of his tongue.

There were fumes coming from her room.

"Stand back," he shouted. "I'm coming in!"

In his prime, he could have kicked in the door. Maybe. But it was a sturdy slab of oak, and that sort of thing always looked easier on TV than it was in reality. So instead of fighting the thing bodily, he used the only leverage he had.

Cursing the growing foul smell, he jammed the blunt end of his cane beneath the door and lifted, trying to pop the thing off its lock, or, failing that, to dislodge a hinge.

The corner lifted slightly, but nothing gave.

"Come on, you bastard!" he shouted, not sure whether he was talking to himself, the door or the man that hunted him.

He shouted again, a wordless cry of rage at the coward who was attacking him through the only two women to touch his life since Celia, and lifted with every shred of power left to him.

The cane gave slightly at the weak point, where the titanium shaft was joined to the molded head by a thin ring of wood he'd taken from his grandfather's walking stick. There was a sharp cracking sound, and the leverage gave.

Erik cursed, thinking he'd broken the cane, then shouted when the door shuddered and popped inward, free of its lock.

Instead of swinging inward, it bumped against something soft.

Erik forced himself to quit breathing as he squeezed through the doorway and saw his worst fears confirmed.

Meg lay near the door, out cold. Or worse.

Eyes streaming with the caustic burn of whatever foulness cloaked the crystal-clear air of her bedroom, he bent and picked her up, nearly losing his pitiful lungful of air when the strain overloaded his back and hip, neither of which was used to heavy lifting anymore.

His physical therapist had told him to hit the gym and strengthen the muscles he had left. At the time, he'd told the PT where to stick her crunches. Now, he wished he'd listened.

He staggered beneath Meg's weight, then steadied himself through force of will. He made it out of the bedroom and into the hall, but the fumes had leaked through the open door and poisoned the atmosphere there, as well. Knowing he had to get her out into the fresh air, Erik descended the steps one at a time while trying to figure out if she was breathing.

He didn't think so.

Her deadweight dragged him down, making him stagger when he hit bottom. He was panting with a combination of exertion, rage and fear by the time he got them to the front door. He opened it somehow, got her outside onto the granite landing somehow, and let her slide to the ground in an ungraceful heap.

Still not breathing.

"Come on, Meg, come *on!*" He felt beneath her T-shirt and found a heartbeat even as he yanked his spare cell phone from his back pocket and punched in 9-1-1. He gave her address along with Peters's name, wanting the detectives in on this one.

What poisoned a room without changing the appearance of the air? How had it gotten into her bedroom after he'd made his search?

Erik cursed and shoved the questions aside. He straightened her sprawl, cleared an airway and tilted her head back slightly, remembering the actions drilled into him so long ago at the academy.

He was vaguely aware of voices and people nearby, of alarmed shouts and prurient neighborly interest, but his whole attention was focused on Meg. On her blue lips and motionless chest.

"Breathe, damn it!" He exhaled as hard as he could, trying to clear the stale, tainted air from his own lungs before he inhaled, bent and touched his lips to hers. He blocked the memory of those lips from the day before, when they'd kissed, then fought. Or rather, when they'd kissed and he'd offered to sleep with her in exchange for the NPT technology.

The memory wasn't a pretty one in the light of day.

Breathe. Breathe. He dimly realized he was chanting the words in between puffs, in between exhalations that left him dizzy for his own ration of air. Then hands were tugging at him, pulling him away from her.

For a moment he thought she was dead, that he had been too late, that they had come to take her body and put it in one of those cold, black bags. He'd been too late to save Jimmy eight years earlier, and now he'd been too late to save Meg.

Too damn late.

"We've got her. It's okay." A woman's face swam into view, square jawed and kind-eyed. When he just stared at her, she gripped his shoulders and eased him away. "You did good. You kept her going. We'll take it from here."

He was dimly aware of a smattering of applause from the gathered bystanders, but the whole of his attention was focused on Meg. On the rise and fall of her chest beneath the oversize T-shirt, and the rose-pink that was edging out the blue of her lips.

Relief seared through him. She was breathing.

As he watched, she coughed weakly and her eyelids fluttered partway open, then sagged shut again.

He let out the breath he hadn't even realized he'd been holding. "She's alive."

"Thanks to you." The female paramedic eased him out of the way as her partner, a younger man with a faintly panicked air of this-is-my-first-day-don't-let-me-kill-anyone, approached with a rolling gurney loaded with a backboard. The woman subtly blocked Erik's view of Meg. "What happened?"

"Fumes," he said tersely, "I don't know what kind. She was unconscious when I found her. She'd been out a minute, maybe more."

She held out a clipboard. "Can you fill in the basics for me?"

He looked down at the sheet, which asked for her age, allergies, next of kin and their contact information. "Her name's Meg Corning. I don't know the other stuff. I'll have to call her boss. They'll have records."

"Okay." The female paramedic took the clipboard back but gave him an odd look. Then again, it was just past eight in the morning, and he'd carried Meg out of her house wearing her PJs. The paramedic had added one plus one and gotten an uncomplimentary two, rather than the reality, which was more like one-and-a-half.

He wasn't an uncaring lover or one-night stand who didn't know the first thing about his bed partner. He was...

Hell, he didn't know anymore.

Detectives Peters and Sturgeon arrived on the heels of two local cops. The four conferred quickly on the sidewalk before approaching the house en masse.

Peters shook Erik's hand, a touch of normalcy that felt out of place against the backdrop of hustling paramedics and lookey-loos on the street. The detective said, "What happened?"

"That's what I'd like to know." As Meg was loaded onto the gurney and strapped in, Erik did his best to sketch the situation for the assembled cops. When he got to the part about the fumes, he shrugged. "I'm no chemicals expert, but it was weird. No smoke or anything in the room, but it was like breathing razor blades. It smelled like—" he frowned, thinking back "—chlorine, maybe? Only it burned like hell." He glanced at the house, which had seemed tight the night before. "I checked the room when we got home. Nothing. How'd he get in? A window? Fiber optics? Something else?"

One of the local cops, a heavyset guy who looked too old to be in uniform without a story, asked, "You want to come in with us?"

It was the respect accorded another cop, rather than a civilian. But although Erik appreciated the gesture and part of him was itching to get back in there, to see what the scene had to tell them, he shook his head. "Thanks, but I think I'll ride to the hospital with Meg."

A single raised eyebrow was Peters's only reaction to his use of her first name.

"We'll be in touch," Sturgeon said, and the older detective gestured the others toward Meg's house as a marked van arrived, bearing one of the private crime scene units subcontracted to the local PD.

"You coming?" the female paramedic called from the open back doors of the ambulance. "She's asking for you."

Those four words loosened something tight and messy in Erik's chest, something that told him he'd almost been too late to save her. He nodded and climbed stiffly to his feet. "Yeah, I'm riding with you."

He took one step toward the street and his leg nearly folded beneath him.

His cane was still upstairs.

A LOW BURN of acid anger choked Edward, nearly doubling him over at the edge of the crowd gathered on the Beacon Hill sidewalk. He couldn't believe it. The bitch had survived. Again.

He had failed. Again.

You didn't fail, a familiar voice whispered in his ear. *Everyone else cheats. They cheat my baby out of*

*what you deserve. You have to make them pay. Make
them pay. Make them pay...*

"Hey, dude. Are you okay?"

The young boy's voice brought Edward's attention back to the matter at hand. He willed his
mother's voice back to the warm, remembering place
where it lived inside his head and nodded at the kid.
"Yeah. I'm fine."

When the boy frowned, looking confused as he
tried to peer past the sweatshirt's hood, Edward
turned and walked away. Away from the house. Away
from the place where they'd cheated him out of his
success.

Or not *they,* really. Falco had been the cheat. If it
hadn't been for him, the plan would have worked
perfectly.

It was Falco's fault.

He would have to be punished.

IT WAS LATE AFTERNOON before Meg managed to
escape from the hospital. She signed herself out
against the doctor's orders, but she figured her
medical degree gave her some perspective on the
situation. She was conscious and alert, and the only
lingering aftereffects of her ordeal were a faint pain
in her chest and a squishy wheezing sound when she
breathed. The latter symptom was improving by the
hour as the drugs helped dry the fluid that had collected in response to the chemical burns.

The hydrochloric acid gas burns, to be exact.

She'd overheard the cops outside her door talking

about it after Erik left to meet with the detectives. Or, more accurately, after Erik snuck out to meet with the detectives, pretending to be headed home for a change of clothes.

She appreciated the effort, if not the deception.

Outside the hospital, dressed in the clothes a white-faced Jemma had brought for her, Meg hailed a taxi. "Chinatown police station, please."

The cabbie glanced at her in the mirror. "There's a closer station if you're in trouble."

Which made her wonder just how bad she looked. "No, thanks. I'm meeting someone." *He just doesn't know it yet.*

The drive from the hospital to the station was a short twenty minutes in the Boston traffic, but that was long enough for butterflies to gather in her gut, pulsing in time with the ache in her chest. She'd gone to bed angry with Erik, convinced that Jemma was right and he was too much work.

She'd awoken to terror, and awoken the second time with his lips on hers, his breath forcing air into her lungs. Certainly life-saving pulmonary resuscitation should tip the scales in his favor, at least a little bit.

Right?

"We're here." The cabbie named his price and she paid with a hefty tip, then hesitated a moment before climbing out.

Here goes nothing.

She wasn't sure why she was so anxious about seeing Erik again, when nothing had really changed.

But her system was revving on nerves by the time the desk officer escorted her to the conference room. The two detectives and Erik stood when she entered, a chivalrous gesture that was ruined when Erik grabbed her arms, turned her to face him and scowled.

"What the hell are you doing here? The doctor said he was keeping you overnight for observation."

She shrugged. "Our opinions differed. I had seniority."

He aimed her for the door. "Come on. I'll take you back."

"Or not." She pulled away, sat and focused on the detectives. "What can you tell me?"

"Nothing," Erik said from the doorway. "You're going back to the hospital."

When she just sat, waiting for the detectives to answer her question, he cursed and retook his seat, grumbling, "I don't know why I'm bothering. My life would be easier if you were out of commission."

"Be careful saying things like that. I might take you seriously." Meg kept her tone light, but couldn't help the faint shiver brought by his words.

Intellectually, she knew he wasn't involved. But in her gut… No, her gut didn't think so, either. He might have motive, but he was a better man than that, whether he believed it or not.

The detectives apparently agreed, because neither of them commented. Instead, Peters said, "We found a crude time delay device beneath your bed." A chill chased through Meg's system as he continued, "He left one of those cardboard-based flowerpots filled with ice, propped up over a petri dish loaded with—" he glanced at his notes "—phosphorous pentachloride. When the ice melted, it soaked through the flowerpot until it—"

"Dripped water into the dish," she finished for him, raising her voice so she could hear herself over the rising buzz in her head. "Water plus phosphorous pentachloride equals hydrogen chloride gas. Vaporized hydrochloric acid."

Yes, she realized in hindsight. That had been the smell. Like the faint vapors that occasionally escaped from the fume hood during experiments involving liquid hydrochloric acid, only a hundred thousand times more deadly.

Erik must have seen the sudden knowledge in her eyes, because he nodded, seeming satisfied that she was good and scared now. "Exposure to the gas can lead to everything from burning eyes, throat and lungs to pulmonary edema, heart failure and death." He glanced at her and a flash of concern supplanted the coolness in his expression. "You sure you should be out of bed?"

His husky voice brought a flash of sensory memory, a wash of heat and the image of him standing beside her if-you-buy-it-he-will-come bed.

She shook her head and willed the thought away. "I'm fine. Do we know how he got in?"

Peters lifted one shoulder in a half shrug. "You don't have the best locks and there's no security system. It wouldn't have been difficult for a savvy amateur lock pick to pop your front door."

"The security company is coming tomorrow," she said, resisting the urge to rub at the gooseflesh that had risen at the thought of someone picking her locks and waltzing into her home. Into her bedroom. "They said they couldn't fit me in earlier than that."

"The locks have already been changed out and the security system will be in by this evening," Erik said, eyes holding a faint challenge as though he expected her to toss the gesture back at him.

But while she might be the stubborn mule her father had once called her, she wasn't stupid. She nodded. "Thank you."

There wasn't much more to the meeting after that beyond a bunch of negatives. No fingerprints. No discernable evidence of the break-in beyond the device under the bed, which had been made from very standard materials—ice, flowerpot, petri dish and chemicals.

"Except that the petri dish and phosphorous pentachloride would argue for someone with access to scientific reagents," Meg said. "Maybe in a drug company."

"Or research," Erik said, but she knew he was just trying to yank her chain. Nobody in academia would commit murder over a licensing agreement. There was enough grant money that most anything could get funded, and the whole point of academia was that it wasn't about the money. It was about the discovery.

Peters shifted in his chair, frustration etching his features. "We've gone over the lists you both provided, and we've got nothing so far. We've got too many suspects with plausible motives, and too few man-hours available to check out each one. We need to narrow things down."

"I have an idea about that," Meg said, but Erik's steely-eyed glare cut her off.

"You weren't included in that 'we,' Dr. Corning." He shifted his attention to the detectives. "I have a few ideas. Nothing solid yet, but some strings to pull, at least. Can you get an officer to run Meg to my place and keep her there until I get back?"

"Wait a minute!" She surged to her feet. "You're not keeping me anywhere. I'm an adult and I'm free to do whatever I want to—"

"Keep yourself safe," he interrupted, standing and facing her as he had done the night before.

And, as it had the night before, tension crackled in the air between them.

When she didn't back down, he sighed. "Please," he said finally. "I'm asking you nicely, as a favor to me, let an officer take you to my place. Lock yourself in. Take a nap. Order food. Order a movie. I don't care what you do as long as you do it somewhere safe."

"Why can't I go back to my place?" she challenged, knowing that wasn't the point but not quite sure what the point was anymore.

"Because the security system won't be finished until later," he said, "and because I'd feel better if I knew you were staying at my place. It's better protected."

She wavered, knowing she could use a few hours'

sleep. "You're awfully worried about my safety for someone who just admitted his life would be easier if I were out of it." She'd meant the words to come out as a challenge. Instead they sounded faintly wistful.

He shot her an unreadable look. "I changed my mind. I decided it's in my best interest to keep you alive until the deal's done, just in case you've conveniently 'forgotten' any little details in the notes you're going to pass over."

Knee-jerk indignation was followed by a surge of hurt, but she fought to show neither. "Thanks for clearing that up. Jerk." She rounded on Peters, who was trying to hide an expression that hovered somewhere between amusement and disgust. "Find me a driver and make sure they know where the jerk lives, because I don't know and I don't care. I won't be going back after this is over."

ERIK LEFT THE STATION with Meg's anger buzzing just beneath his skin. He could've handled that better, but what was he supposed to say? *Stay safe because this morning I thought you were dead and I can't go through that again* sounded weird and clingy, and probably had more to do with Jimmy's death than anything. It had seemed more natural to blame it on the NPT deal, on the distrust he was having trouble sustaining.

Or so he'd told himself. But her inadvertent flinch of hurt hadn't felt good.

Then again, what *had* made him feel good lately?

The job had started to lose its luster. Each acquisition had to outstrip the last until now they were so huge he had nothing tangible to hold on to. His family didn't know what to make of him, his cop friends had drifted back to their own kind and it wasn't as though he made friends with the owners of the companies he snapped up.

No, he realized as he turned away from the heart of Chinatown and gimped his way up the street, headed toward Boston General, he hadn't made many friends in his current life. And of the few he'd made, the one he'd believed in the most, the one he'd depended on…he'd let her down.

Raine had been his conscience and his confidante, helping him remember that the purest of scientific motives would do him no good if he forgot about the individuals working for the companies he acquired. He'd leaned on her, depended on her, liked her. Even trusted her.

Part of him wished he could have loved her. That would have made things much simpler.

"Simple's never been your strong suit," he said out loud. If he'd been into simple, he would've followed eight generations of Falcos into the family business. He would've married one of the five debutantes his mother and aunt had picked for him, to "make sure he had a choice, of course." He wouldn't have become a cop, wouldn't have worked with a snitch named Celia, wouldn't have believed her when she'd said that she loved him, that she wanted to go straight so she'd be worthy of him.

If he'd been into simple, he wouldn't be standing on the sidewalk, propped up on one and a half legs and a titanium cane, staring at the door to one of the last places he wanted to be right then.

But because he'd never done things the simple way, he cursed and pushed through the door into Otto's Climbing Emporium.

Luke Cannon was waiting for him, leaning on the registration desk with a casualness that belied his handicap.

Sure, Cannon would probably call it a "challenge," or maybe a "slight inconvenience." But Erik called it like he saw it. Cannon was handicapped. So was he.

But they weren't there to bond over limps and war stories. Cannon worked for Pentium Pharmaceuticals, the last big company vying for the NPT deal.

Erik crossed to him, more conscious of his gimp than he should have been. "Cannon. Thanks for meeting me. You want to get a drink? Maybe a bite to eat?" Erik's stomach chose that moment to growl, reminding him that his last meal had been a long time ago.

But Cannon shook his head. "No food. Let's climb."

Erik shook his head. "Let's not." *Hell, no!* "I'm here for information about the Pentium bid on Meg's technology, and to figure out what it's going to take to get your people to drop out." He'd decided to go with full-frontal honesty rather than the sort of sneak attack Cannon probably expected.

The sneak attack would come later.

Cannon merely grinned and held up a collection of nylon straps and heavy carabiners. "If you want me to talk, then you're going to have to climb." His grin widened. "Don't worry. I'll—ahem—walk you through it."

It was a dare, a bribe and a threat all rolled into one.

Despite the faint clutch of unease—at the thought of falling, of embarrassing himself, of looking more crippled than he really was—Erik considered his options, which boiled down to the fact that he didn't have an option.

He nodded shortly. "Let's climb."

Chapter Ten

Twenty minutes later Erik wasn't sure which was worse—the fact that he was barely ten feet above floor level on the basic climbing wall, or the fact that he was almost scared. Not of falling onto the padded floor below—he was strapped in, attached to securely set pitons and had Otto on the belay.

No, he was afraid of looking like an idiot.

Since when did he worry about appearances? Since when was he afraid to take a risk for fear of looking silly?

"Since now," he said, realizing that for the first time since he'd fired the annoying physical therapist who'd leaned way too hard on the "therapy" side of things, he was doing something outside his physical comfort zone.

His recent efforts to keep Meg alive didn't count. Nobody worried about looking stupid under life and death circumstances.

"Concentrate on the wall, Falco. Get out of your head," Cannon's voice ordered. He swung near, moving smoothly from foam blob to artificial crevice, seeming not to notice or care that the titanium shaft of his artificial climbing leg made him look like Arnold in the first *Terminator* movie, at the end when he'd started losing flesh.

Erik was immediately shamed by the thought. Besides, what did that make him? He wasn't bionic. He was merely broken.

"This is stupid," he said, clinging grimly to the wall. "My arms hurt and this harness is chafing my ass. How about we call it quits and find that drink?"

"That's not the answer and you know it." Cannon's eyes reflected a sympathy that chafed worse than the nylon harness. "The straps are rubbing because you were too stubborn to borrow gym shorts and your arms are hurting because you've let yourself get soft. You going to add quitter to that list?"

Anger flared. "Why don't you take your climbing harness and—"

"You want to know where Pentium stands on the NPT sale? Then meet me at the top." And with that, Cannon was gone, climbing easily on one leg of flesh, one of alloy metal.

Erik leaned back and looked up. Way up. Probably another fifty or sixty feet up.

"Oh, hell." His stomach tightened on a mix of ego and fear. This could be a trap. Cannon could be in league with the bastard trying to force him to ditch the NPT sale. Hell, he could *be* the bastard. Once they were at the top of the wall, one "faulty" carabiner and a quick shove, and the Falco takeover bid would be finished.

Erik looked down at the padded floor, where Otto stood in his musclebound glory. The gym owner held Erik's belay rope in both hands, nominally ready to take up the slack or to brace against a fall, but his attention was focused on a trio of coeds wearing midriff-baring shirts and butt-hugging shorts.

As though sensing his new climber's gaze, Otto turned and looked at Erik. The gym owner raised one eyebrow and glanced up the wall, to where Cannon was nearly halfway along. Then he returned his gaze to Erik and raised the other eyebrow.

The challenge was clear. *You going or not?*

Erik told himself it had nothing to do with the lilt in Meg's laughter when she'd joked with Otto, nothing to do with the coeds down below or the other climbers, or even the faint pity in Cannon's eyes. It had everything to do with the case and the danger to Raine and Meg.

But even as he told himself that and began to climb, he knew it wasn't quite the truth. It was about the case, yes, but it was also about him.

He was no quitter.

Muttering under his breath, he let go of the foam blobs one at a time and wiped his damp palms on his tan cotton pants, which probably did look ridiculous beneath the climbing harness, but were better than showing off the scarred mess of his leg. Grip restored, he ran through Cannon's basic instructions in his mind. *Keep your center of gravity close to the wall. Plan ahead. Test your hand- and footholds. Check your pitons. Don't foul your belay.*

"Oh, is that all?" He glowered, then craned his neck, looking for the next highest blob. Once he had that, he lifted his bad leg and used the toe of his borrowed climbing shoes to feel for purchase, either a blob or a crack. He was so used to thinking of that leg as deadwood, as a brace akin to his cane, that it took concentrated effort to think about his foot as anything but a prop. It was nearly a full minute before his toe caught on something and held.

Test your foothold. He dug around until it felt secure, then looked up at his chosen handhold, about three feet above him and to the right. This was where it got tricky, regardless of what Cannon said about trusting his body and the laws of inertia. He needed to push off his bad leg and get enough height to snag that handhold.

Which would explain how he'd stalled ten feet up in the first place. There were only two options now— leap or quit.

Erik bit off a curse, pushed off his bad leg and leaped.

THE COP Peters had tagged to escort Meg to her supposed safe hiding spot must've talked to Erik. Or else he was the naturally suspicious type. Either way, he kept a sharp eye on her during the entirety of the hour-long trip.

Not that she was looking for a chance to slip away or anything.

When they finally reached Erik's place in one of the chichi suburbs west of Boston, Meg was surprised to find a modest two-level saltbox on a nicely landscaped lot in a family oriented neighborhood. The pressed-brick driveway and the stonework of the front entrance spoke of money, but the effect was far from ostentatious.

Then again, why had she imagined a mansion? He was a bachelor who, by his own admission, spent more time on the cot in his office than at his home. He had no need for a big place. But in her experience, the practicalities rarely mattered when it came to showing wealth. Her mother, for instance, had wanted half a dozen fancy cars, a pool and three weeks on the Cape each summer. Her father had wanted to be left alone with his research.

These days, they both had what they wanted and seemed happy, but Meg had always wondered what would've happened if they'd thought about compromise.

"Ma'am?" The officer held out his hand. "I'll need the key and the security codes."

She nearly groaned at being ma'am-ed, which made her feel about a hundred years old, and groaned again when she realized she didn't know how long they'd been sitting at the apex of the circular brick driveway, near the front entrance to Erik's house.

She'd zoned out. Then again, she was working on too much stress and not enough sleep. She probably deserved a moment of staring into space.

"I've got it." She opened the cruiser door and hauled herself upright. Residual tightness tugged in her lungs and throat, reminding her that she was damn lucky to have escaped so easily.

Damn lucky Erik had been there to rescue her. Again.

The knowledge fisted beneath her heart, creating a little bubble of nerves when she mounted the front steps and fished in her pocket for the key and security codes he'd given her. The nerves didn't come from fear—she had a cop at her back, after all. They came from the fact that she was venturing into Erik's personal space when everything personal between them was so unsettled.

Knowing there was a certain naughty thrill in that, she unlocked the door and typed in the two-layer security code, one on a unit outside the door, one on a keypad hidden inside the hallway closet.

Normally, she might have wondered what he was trying to hide, but with her own home security proven pitifully inadequate, she was simply grateful.

She turned to the cop. "Are you coming in?"

He shook his head. "No, ma'am. Detective Sturgeon arranged for a local car to swing by every half hour or so." He gestured to Erik's keychain. "Use the panic button if you need it."

She glanced at the fob, a black plastic square with a bright red button in the center. "That'll call 9-1-1 for me?"

"Yes, ma'am." He backed up until he was framed in the open doorway. "I'll wait outside while you lock up and reset the alarms. Wave from the window when you're secure."

Feeling almost foolish, Meg did as she was told. Then she felt even more foolish, because once the cruiser was gone from the driveway and she was alone in Erik's house, she found herself near tears.

The accumulated stresses of the past two weeks felt as if they were crashing down around her all at once. Part of her wanted to curl up in a ball and weep.

But because she was better than that, stronger than that, she went exploring instead.

IT TOOK ERIK a torturous half hour to reach the top of the climbing wall. The route—or "send," as Cannon had called it—got tougher the higher he climbed, with blobs and cracks spaced farther and farther apart. At one point, he'd hit a dead end and had to backtrack, wasting nearly ten minutes.

But he hadn't quit.

Finally he'd used one shaking, sore leg—he wasn't even sure which one was the bad one anymore, they both felt like jelly—to boost himself up and over, onto a three-foot ledge that ran the length of the building, sixty-some feet up.

Cursing, he'd dragged himself onto the flat surface, breathing hard, nearly sniveling with exertion.

"Doesn't look so hard from the ground, does it?" Cannon said. He was sitting a few yards away with his mismatched legs dangling over the edge. He looked cucumber-cool, as though he could lead a high-powered board meeting anytime.

Erik thought about pushing him off for general spite—knowing his belay buddy would break the fall. But that would've taken too much effort, so instead he dragged himself to a sitting position beside the other man. "I'm up here. Now talk."

"Look around you." Cannon gestured to the upper levels of the climbing gym, where the original floors of the warehouse had been gutted and replaced with tall beams, making the place feel like a pillared coliseum. The padded floor seemed far away, the other people small and unimportant. "Now picture open air. Just rocks and sky and a few climbing buddies. And tell me this isn't worth a little butt chafe."

Erik grimaced and ignored a faint, wistful memory of hiking with his granddad, back before everything had gotten so complicated in the family. "I don't need a hobby, I need information. Where does Pentium stand on the NPT deal?"

"We're out."

It took a moment for the words to penetrate, another for the irritation to rise. "You brought me all the way up here to tell me that? And what the hell do you mean, you're out? It's going to be a huge breakthrough!"

Cannon shrugged. "True, but the head honchos think the ethics may be a tad squidgy—it's based on stem cells, after all, and fair or not, that raises the whole specter of experimenting on human embryos.

After that brouhaha last year when our steroid testing kits gave false positives on a half dozen of baseball's finest, and the class-action lawsuit the year before, we're trying to keep a low profile."

"The ethics are fine," Erik said. "But don't let me talk you into it. I'd just as soon Pentium stayed out of the mix."

"Then you're in luck." Cannon turned his attention back to the open space surrounding them. "And you already know why I made you climb up here to get your precious answer. You needed to climb."

"Bull. I need to finish this deal before I—" Erik broke off. "Never mind. How the hell do we get down?"

He wasn't looking for a friend, wasn't looking to bounce his problems off a near stranger. Though he was willing to bet that Cannon was on the up-and-up, and that he'd told the truth about Pentium's status in the NPT deal, that didn't make them buddies.

"We rappel." Cannon briefly outlined the procedure, and then was gone, leaping out into open space tethered only by his main line and the safety belay. He swung in and pushed off the wall once, twice, three times, his artificial leg making a weird, mechanical sound as it absorbed the shock.

Determined to ignore the twist of nerves in his stomach and the raw chafe of his harness, Erik double-checked his attachment point, muttered something uncomplimentary about Cannon, and pushed himself off the ledge while letting the rope play through.

He was braced for pain when he swung in and pushed off. There was pain, yes, a singing jolt of impact that ricocheted up both legs. But that sensation was lost in another.

The feeling of flying.

It only took a handful of seconds for him to reach the ground. A few heartbeats. One slow exhale. But it was long enough to remind him of the rush of speed and wind and adrenaline he'd once craved, once lived for.

In that moment, he remembered himself.

Then he hit the padded floor too fast. His bad leg howled pain and buckled, and he fell off to one side. When he reached out to catch himself, his arms fouled the lines.

He landed on his face. In public. The crash helmet Cannon had pressed on him absorbed most of the impact, but pain thrummed from his heels to the top of his head. He groaned and rolled onto his back just in time to watch a small crowd gather.

Otto looked sheepish. "Sorry, dude. I thought you had it under control." Translation—he'd been flirting with the coeds.

A strange woman bent close. "Are you okay?"

"He's fine," Cannon said. He shooed the others away and tossed Erik's cane, so it landed a few feet away. "And don't tell me it hurts. If it doesn't hurt, you're not pushing yourself hard enough."

He walked away, headed for the locker room on one flesh leg, one metallic one.

Erik cursed Cannon, cursed his relatives and any

children who might be unlucky enough to have the heartless bastard as their father. Then he pushed himself up, stripped off that godawful harness and hauled himself to his feet. His legs were shaking— both of them—and he was soaked with sweat, but there was no way he was getting naked in a communal shower, so he headed for the door, pausing only to pay for the dubious pleasure of using the wall, the rental equipment and Otto's so-called spotting.

"You're all set." The gum-popping girl at the front desk waved him past. "Luke took care of it."

Erik nodded curtly and stalked past.

He tried to tell himself that he'd achieved his goal, that they could cross Pentium off their suspect list, because why would they care who bought NPT if they weren't still in the running for the deal?

But as he hit the street and the sharp fall air chilled the damp shirt to his back, he found himself thinking not of the case, but of Meg waiting for him in his house. On his turf. Surrounded by his things.

He wasn't sure what to call the emotion that rattled in his chest. Wariness, maybe, or fascination. But as he collected his Mercedes, her image was firmly in the forefront of his mind, along with Cannon's parting words.

If it doesn't hurt, you're not pushing yourself hard enough.

THE WAY MEG SAW IT, there was a pretty fuzzy line between scientific curiosity and plain nosiness. She figured she'd stepped over that line the moment she moved out of Erik's living room and into his high-tech office. But the door was open, and he hadn't told her any part of the house was off limits, had he?

Okay, she was rationalizing, but something compelled her to cross the vibrantly patterned Oriental rug and slide into the soft leather chair behind his desk. A desire to understand Erik, perhaps, or the effect he had on her.

They were on opposite sides of a pitched battle. He was the enemy, representing the big business and industry her father had warned her against for so many years. And Erik was no prize on the personal level, either. He was suspicious and reactive, and wanted to blame her for an attraction that clearly went both ways.

"Why do I always pick the complicated ones?" she said, thinking back to her two past serious relationships. She had to think back a ways, to before she started working at BoGen.

Benjamin had been a fellow grad student who'd shared her enthusiasm for the extreme outdoors. He'd had a mean, jealous streak she'd ignored for the most part, but when he'd quit school to "find himself," she hadn't been at all tempted by his offer of a shared sleeping bag in Alaska.

After him had been Foster, a stockbroker who worked long hours and liked fine wine and fast airplanes. It had taken her nearly three months to figure out that he'd also liked juggling girlfriends. What she'd thought were his deep, reflective silences were actually moments when he was scrambling to remember his cover story.

At least Ben and Foster had been kind to her, for the most part. Erik hadn't even bothered with that much. Then again, maybe that made him more honest than most, in an antisocial sort of way.

"Face it," she said out loud, "you want him, but you don't always like him."

Rather than echoing back, her words were deadened by the pleated blinds covering the single, wide window, and the built-in shelves that held everything from paperback novels to a wooden ship model in an expensive-looking glass case.

The ship seemed out of place, a touch of whimsy in an otherwise utilitarian workspace.

Aware that she was invading his privacy and not sure she cared, not even sure what she was looking for, Meg slid a stack of folders from one side of his desk to the other. She murmured, "Well, well. What have we here?"

The motion had revealed a framed picture tucked into a corner alcove.

The photo was grainy with age, and the six clustered figures wore clothes from another decade, in styles that had already come and gone at least once more in the years since. The picture showed what looked like three generations, with an older man standing behind a smiling couple in their thirties, with three boys, dark haired and happy, arranged in the foreground. The quality of the outdated clothes spoke of wealth, as did the marina in the background, where a large sailboat called the *Amadeus* lay berthed.

Meg couldn't find Erik's adult features in the faces of the three boys, who ranged in age from probably nine or ten to midteens, but she had to guess it was his family portrait. It seemed strange to think of Erik as having brothers, and she shrugged off the faint twist of envy she habitually felt at the thought of siblings. She would have liked a brother or sister, but her parents had been too intent on their separate goals.

Would things have been different between her parents if they'd had more children? Would her mother have felt compelled to stay then? She stared at the photo, trying to force the answer, but there was nothing but six static smiles and a twinkle of humor in the old man's eyes.

"This is getting me nowhere." Though she was almost reluctant to set it aside, she tucked the photo back where she'd found it before she rose and began pacing the room. She wouldn't turn on the computer—that would be taking the snooping thing too far—but there had to be something in here that would give her leverage when it came to dealing with Erik on the professional level.

And maybe the personal one, a thoughtlet whispered in her brain, and for a change she didn't shove it away. *Yeah,* she agreed mentally, *maybe the personal one.*

But when she finally found her leverage tucked behind the model ship, it was nothing like what she'd expected, and nothing she could, in good conscience, use in the negotiations.

But it sure explained a hell of a lot.

ON HIS WAY HOME, Erik phoned the detectives to let them know that Pentium had moved down to his "probably not" list, and to see if they had come up with anything.

"Nothing on the trace evidence from Dr. Corning's home," Peters said, frustration edging his tone. "This guy is either damn good or damn lucky." There was a pause and the sound of rustling paper. "The techs came up with a possibility on the security videos from the hospital, though. Looks like a young man, late teens, early twenties, wearing loose jeans, a dark sweatshirt and a skullcap. The video caught him walking away from the elevator just after it fell."

"That doesn't sound very concrete," Erik said as he pulled off the highway, headed for his place in the 'burbs.

"True, except that we can't find him entering the building."

That got Erik's attention. "All the entrances are videoed?"

"Yes, and my people are good. We've got a decent shot of the lower half of his face, and new recognition software on beta-testing from the feds. We can't find him entering the hospital that day or five days prior."

"No ID?"

"Not yet. We're having to extrapolate the upper

half from averages, and haven't hit on anything. But when we showed the picture around, one of the construction workers recognized him. Said he threw the kid off the site the day Dr. Corning went into the cement form."

Ice sluiced through Erik's veins. "And he's just telling you this now?"

"Said he'd forgotten all about it until he saw the picture. Sadly, that's life with eyewitnesses."

"You looking for the punk?"

"Of course, but you know how it is."

"Right." Contrary to the popular media's view of police work, it wasn't easy to find someone who didn't want to be found. "You want to fax me a copy of that picture?" Erik asked, knowing Peters wouldn't have shared info if he hadn't been planning to do just that.

"It's on its way. You headed home?"

"Yeah. Did the locals report anything hinky?"

"Nothing," Peters said. "She didn't try to sneak out, and nobody tried to get in."

"Thanks." An invisible band loosened from around Erik's chest. Part of him had expected Meg to climb out the window and take off, just to prove she could.

Then again, maybe it was a bad sign she hadn't tried it. Maybe it meant—

Nothing. It didn't meant a thing. She was who she was, nothing more, nothing less.

The detective's voice gained a note of finality when he said, "Call me if there's anything I should know."

"Same goes," Erik said before he disconnected the call. But both of them knew the Chinatown detectives would share exactly as much as they wanted to. Erik wasn't a cop anymore.

Wouldn't be one ever again.

The brief thought reminded him of the climbing wall. Eight years earlier, he would've climbed it without a harness and laughed at the simplicity. That afternoon, it had taken him nearly an hour, and he was already feeling the burn of sore muscles.

He shouldn't feel ridiculously pleased that he'd made it to the top and back again. Because he did, and because he wasn't yet ready to lose that feeling, he tucked it away for future reference. When this was over, maybe he'd try physical therapy again. Hell, maybe he'd skip right over PT and just start pushing himself.

Then he turned into his driveway and thoughts of the climbing wall fled at the sight of lit windows and the shadow of a woman passing from one room to the next on the lower floor.

The cop in him cringed at the easy target she presented, though their perp had yet to use a firearm. But the man in him focused on her outline, on the strong, womanly curves that sometimes became lost beneath the force of her personality, the stress of the situation.

Meg was a beautiful woman.

But she's not for you, his saner self reminded him. *You're not for her.*

"I know," he said, but that knowledge didn't stop

him from wishing he looked neater, smelled cleaner and moved faster as he parked the car and climbed the front steps. It didn't stop him from thinking that this was the first time he'd felt anticipation as he reached for the doorknob of his own house.

He was gratified to find it locked and to find the outer keypad armed and beaming a solid red light. He tapped in the required code and used his spare key, then tapped in the second code in the coat closet, resetting both alarms. With some thought of letting her know he'd arrived and then heading straight upstairs to shower, he stuck his head around the corner, into the living room, knowing he'd last seen her silhouette heading toward the kitchen.

The smell of cooking—rosemary and something warm—punched straight to his gut with its unexpectedness, sending him back a step into the marble foyer.

When was the last time he'd come home to cooking? Not since that last night with Celia. Before that, he had to go back to the years B.C.—Before Cop—when the invitations to family functions had still arrived regularly, when he'd felt comfortable going home for Sunday dinner with the 'rents, his older brothers and their families. Back when his grandfather had been alive and his family had at least made an effort to understand why he couldn't be like them.

Meg appeared in the doorway separating the U-shaped kitchen from the foyer, and stopped dead. "You're home!" She lifted a hand to her throat, then dropped it to fiddle with a dishtowel she'd tucked in the waistband of her business-like black trousers. She wore the tailored white blouse she'd had on earlier in the day, but had discarded the soft green blazer and her tall black boots. A tentative smile touched her lips. "I didn't hear you come in."

"You made dinner."

The flatness of his words dimmed something in her eyes. "Yes. I needed to keep myself busy. To keep moving. Otherwise…" She gestured to the world beyond the sensored windows, dark now with the quick fall night. "I hope you don't mind that I snooped in your cabinets for food and pans."

A shadow moved through her expression, there and gone so fast he almost missed it. But he caught it, and the fleeting, furtive glimpse put him on guard. The smell of food gained a scheming edge.

"It's fine. Smells good." Reduced to monosyllables, he gestured upstairs. "I'm going to grab a quick shower."

"A fax came for you. A picture."

He nodded. "They think that's the guy. Recognize him?"

"No. I wish I did. It would make more sense, be more…reasonable in a way, not like any of this is reasonable."

Her guarded expression told him that by "this" she didn't only mean the attacks, but also the tension that had snapped into the fragrant air between them, along with the cooking smells.

"I'll be down in a few minutes," he said. "We'll talk then."

He stumped up the stairs and tried to ignore the growing howl in his leg. The long unused bottle of painkillers in the master bath beckoned, but he didn't dare. He needed to keep his mind sharp.

Because one thing was clear to him. She hadn't cooked just to keep herself busy. She'd cooked to soften him up.

She wanted something.

Chapter Eleven

Meg retreated to the kitchen, to the familiar acts of checking the sautéed veggies and sauce, and boiling water for the pasta she'd found. Erik's plentiful food stores indicated that he either cooked or had someone cook for him, but almost everything was dried, boxed or frozen for the long haul, suggesting that his cooking schedule was erratic at best.

That fit with what she knew of the man. He was driven. He slept in his office as often as she slept in the lab.

And now she knew why.

Her fingers faltered, sending the lid clattering onto the heating pan of water.

"It doesn't change anything," she said, but she strained to hear the shower upstairs as her brain reviewed the sparse, sensationalized details she'd found in a newspaper clipping in Erik's office.

No wonder the detectives were cutting him an unusual amount of slack on the current case. Lieutenant Erik Falco had been a damned hero.

She heard an uneven footstep upstairs. She'd peeked into the master bath earlier and stepped out immediately, unsettled by the basic masculinity of the black-and-green marble and the scent in the air, a mix of soap and attitude. But it had been the sight of the prescription painkillers—sealed over, unopened— that had unnerved her the most, mute testimony to a life he hadn't chosen, a pain he fought daily.

How could she not respect that? How could she not—

"Your water's boiling."

At the sound of Erik's voice in the doorway, Meg squeaked and spun, face flaming suddenly hot when she realized he'd been watching her, and hotter still when she saw the glitter in his eyes. She wasn't sure whether it was irritation or attraction, but there was no mistaking the growing tension between them, the wary intimacy of being alone together in the big, sturdy house with police patrols on the half hour and motion sensors on the doors and windows.

She stared at him, seeing that his shower-wet hair was roughened to damp spikes where he'd toweled it dry. He wore another of his button-down shirts, though this one was soft with a lack of starch, and hung untucked over a pair of faded jeans. His feet were bare, his jaw unshaven, giving him the look of a wealthy playboy relaxing at home.

Which wasn't far wrong, aside from the playboy part. She doubted he'd played in a long time. It wasn't in the nature of the man she'd come to know over the past week.

The man she'd come to desire. To need.

The truth of it drove her back a step, away from where he stood motionless, leaning against the door frame in a pose that was part casual, part necessity. He could have been framing himself for a photo shoot, an ad for jeans maybe, or an expensive, gritty cologne. Something sexy and masculine and self-possessed.

He arched one eyebrow. "The water?"

"Right." She forced herself to focus on the simple act of guesstimating two people's worth of pasta. She told herself she could handle this. She could—

"What's wrong?" His voice spoke from too close behind her. She stiffened and he continued, "You seem nervous. Did something happen?"

Yes, something had happened, but not the way he meant. Not having to do with the danger that threatened from outside, seeming further away than the night beyond the windows. Something had shifted inside her. It felt sudden, but maybe it wasn't sudden at all. Maybe it had been building for the past five days, ever since he'd entered her office and she'd found herself attracted to a married man who wasn't married at all.

"Nothing's wrong," she said, telling herself it was the truth. She stirred the pasta and set the timer for the quick boil. Then, not having anything else mundane and cooking-related to focus on, she turned to face Erik.

Sure enough, he was too close, standing in the

middle of the marble-and-granite kitchen, which was done in a warm brown but had seemed sterile and unfriendly when she'd first set foot inside. Now, redolent with the smell of sauce and garlic bread, filled with the presence of the man opposite her, the space seemed anything but sterile.

It felt hot and dangerous. Tempting. Almost like the last few seconds before a free fall, when she used to pause on the threshold between airplane and air, feeling a moment of panic just before she jumped.

She looked up into his eyes, which were higher than she remembered. He was taller than her original perception. Broader. Stronger.

He'd needed to be.

Something of the knowledge must have shown in her eyes, because his darkened and he backed off a step and cursed. "You snooped."

She'd expected to feel embarrassed, but instead she felt a strange bubble of heat, of laughter. "Of course I did. What did you expect?"

"I—" He broke off, furrowed his brow and paused a moment before he said, "Hell, I don't know. Maybe I figured you'd find it. Maybe on some level I wanted you to before…" He shrugged. "Before something happened between us that you'd regret later."

She leaned back against the counter beside the stove, surprised by his admission and by the additional heat it had stirred. "Tell me about the picture in your office."

His eyes clouded momentarily, then cleared, though they remained somber. "The picture. I'd forgotten."

She suspected that wasn't quite the truth, given the lack of dust on the tucked-away frame, but she waited while their dinner cooked at her back.

"I was the youngest," he finally said, a faint smile ghosting his lips. "My brothers called me the runt of the litter."

His expression didn't invite questions, but she didn't care. Something about the photograph, about the fact that he'd had only that one old shot, had set off warning buzzers in her scientist's brain. "Are you close to them now?"

He shrugged. "Not particularly. An annual holiday phone call. That's about it. My brothers have their families. My parents have their travel. And my grandfather passed a few years ago."

He shifted his weight and lifted his cane to eye level, so she could see the thin ring of dark wood set into the metal barrel. Then he shook his head and dropped it again. "No. We're not close. They didn't understand why I wanted to be a cop. There wasn't ever a big fight, but over time we sort of...drifted." He shrugged. "It happens."

"I know." But though she'd certainly drifted when it came to her parents, Meg didn't understand how that could happen between siblings. What about the bonds of childhood, of shared experiences? Shared ages and blood?

The timer went off, interrupting and giving her an outlet for the sudden buzz of energy, of restless motion that skittered through her, sending her for the plates she'd set out already. She drained the pasta and dumped it in with the sauce, then added grated cheese and a dash of oil.

"Sit. I'll bring it to you." She gestured to a small, round table set into a windowed alcove at the back of the kitchen.

Hours earlier, she'd decided to skip the stiff formality of the dining room and use the more comfortable, casual kitchen table. At the time, she'd told herself she was thanking him for the use of his place, for saving her butt, and for having been a cop in a situation she couldn't even imagine. But now she realized the table had another advantage. Or was it a disadvantage?

The tiny alcove was an intimate space, an enclosure that would have their knees bumping. She hadn't set out a candle when she'd put out the mats and silverware, but with the stained-glass chandelier turned low, she might as well have. The overall effect was one of romance. Seduction.

When she realized that, she also realized he hadn't moved. He remained standing in the center of the warm brown kitchen, eyes suspicious. "What do you want from me?"

Irritation flared alongside the simmering heat from the stove, from the man. "I don't *want* anything. Not the way you mean it. I wanted to thank you for letting me crash, for helping me even when you don't particularly like me."

"I like you just fine," he muttered, and turned for the table, shoulders stiff.

"Be still my heart." But she grinned as she said it.

Then she took a deep breath. "I found the newspaper clipping. The one about how you were injured."

That stopped him dead in his tracks, but he didn't turn. His voice was muffled with distance and something else when he said, "And your answer was spaghetti?"

"My answer was to do something nice for you. I don't get the impression you've had much of that lately."

Now he turned, expression closed. "I have everything I need and enough money to buy most anything I want."

The sentiment was her mother's, but the look in his eye wasn't as sure as the words. That was enough to send her forward a step. Remembering the stark newsprint that had described a hostage situation, a police shootout and a partner killed in the line of duty, she touched his arm. "Sit and eat. A meal between a man and a woman. It doesn't need to be any more complicated than that."

Instead of sitting, he looked from the table to the stove to her. His stillness was almost awful in its intensity. "The last woman who cooked me an intimate meal was one of my contacts, back when I was a cop. We shouldn't have gotten involved—it was stupid of me. Hormones, maybe, or that sense of invincibility I should've outgrown after a few years on the force. That last night, she fed me, took me to bed and told me she loved me. The next day, my partner and I walked into an ambush."

Meg's blood chilled in her veins. "She was

killed?" The clipping hadn't mentioned another casualty, but there was death in his eyes.

"She set me up," he said flatly, not looking away, but not seeing her, either. "She used me to feed information to the department, information her bastard boyfriend wanted us to have." He laughed, a harsh sound that held more self-loathing than humor. "The chief didn't want to trust her, but I pushed. 'She'll be useful,' I said. 'I can control her.' Yeah, right. She was the one in control all along, and I was too caught up in the sex to see it."

Meg didn't say a thing. She was surprised to learn that sympathy and jealous anger could coexist with such force, as they battled for dominance in her chest. In her soul.

It shouldn't matter that he'd loved the woman who had betrayed him. The betrayal explained much about him, about the deep, dark suspicion that had clouded too many of their interactions over the past week. He'd been burned, and a friend had died. No wonder he held himself aloof.

Though she hadn't spoken, he nodded. "Yeah. I was stupid. She fed me a few real tips, enough so we bagged some low-level scumbags—street dealers and yuppie users, mostly. Disposable assets that hinted at the bigger score. That night, between the salad-in-a-bag and the meat loaf, she told me she had something bigger, something she'd only pass along if I promised to protect her, promised to get her out of the life." He laughed, again without joy or mirth. "I told her she didn't have to buy me, that I'd get her out the instant she gave the word, but she insisted on helping me set up the big score. So we could start on even footing, she said."

He fell silent then. Meg was aware of the fading warmth of the stove at her back. She wanted to touch him, to tell him he didn't have to keep going. She'd already heard more than enough.

Instead, sensing that he hadn't talked about it in far too long, she said, "You didn't know. You couldn't have known."

"That's not good enough," he said harshly, then took a deep breath. "She said there was going to be a big delivery in broad daylight, near a busy intersection downtown. It was just weird enough to ring true, and of course I believed her. She said she loved me."

It was on the tip of Meg's tongue to ask if he'd loved her in return, but she held the words in, not sure she wanted to know either way. If he'd loved the other woman, it meant he was capable of love, or had been at one time. If he hadn't loved her, then the betrayal had been one of trust, not emotion. But either way, the experience had changed him, and not for the better. It had left him closed off. Inaccessible. It had set him on her mother's path, one of money over family. It would be foolish for her to go back to a place she'd already been.

Yet she found herself saying, "Tell me."

He sent her a hooded glance, one that was made dangerous by the hint of stubble at his jawline and the awful tension that vibrated through his frame. He said, "We put a team on the drop point and manned the surrounding areas, but we didn't have anyone in the bank on the corner. Stupid oversight. Once the bastards spotted us—exactly where they'd been told to look, though we didn't know it at the time—they bolted into the bank like they'd planned it. Which they had."

He blew out a breath and spread his hands away from his sides, one empty palm up, the other holding his cane. "They took hostages and started shooting before we could get SWAT mobilized."

He fell silent, but Meg could fill in the rest from the article she'd found in his office. A group of cops had feinted toward the front of the building while two others snuck in the back. One wound up dead, the other wounded, but the chaos had been enough for the main team to storm the place and subdue the gunmen.

He nodded as though she'd sketched the events out loud. "Jimmy was a good man. He had a wife and a kid. I hear they're okay now, or as good as could be expected."

"And the woman? The one who betrayed you?"

"In jail," he said flatly. "Doesn't matter, though. Won't bring Jim back. Won't fix my leg."

Something tweaked at Meg when he said that. The way his eyes slid to hers and away, maybe, or the darkness in his voice when he spoke of his injury. But the small, unformed doubt couldn't compete with the surge of tenderness that rose when she saw his closed, unhappy expression, the spike of something hotter and almost protective that grew when she tried to imagine what it had been like. How would she feel if she'd trusted a man who not only betrayed her, but hurt—even killed—someone she cared for? Jemma, maybe, or Max, or even her father?

She'd feel guilty. Ashamed. Angry at the guy who'd set her up. At the world that let things like that happen.

Now she did touch Erik, laying her hand on his forearm, where tendons and muscles thrummed tight beneath shirt and skin. She wanted to soothe him, to tell him it wasn't his fault, but they both knew that on some level it was. He'd trusted the wrong person, and he and his partner had paid the price.

So instead, she forced a grin and said, "It's just spaghetti, but if it's freaking you out, we could order Chinese or something."

Finally, the awful tension eased from his shoulders. "Yeah. Guess I really know how to bring down a room, huh?"

She squeezed his arm, too aware of the warm male flesh beneath her fingertips. "S'okay. This hasn't exactly been a normal week."

They stood there for a few heartbeats, caught in a moment of easy accord so unlike their usual edgy tension. Then he said, "Thanks, Doc. You're okay." Then he bent and kissed her on the lips—

And the easiness vanished.

He might have meant it as a casual peck, an acknowledgment that if they weren't friends, they weren't precisely enemies, either. But the first moment of contact, that first rush of heat, brought her straight back to the conference room and kisses that had been nothing chaste and everything she had wanted.

She parted her lips, partly in shock, partly in invitation. He did the same, but he didn't advance, didn't retreat. Instead he stayed still, barely breathing.

Meg opened her eyes—not even sure when they had closed—and found him looking at her from a few inches away. He didn't say the words, but she could see the question in his eyes. They either stopped now or they didn't stop at all.

The heat curled around them, binding them together in an unseen net of electric attraction. But his stillness reminded her that it wasn't an unbreakable net. They could back away, retreat from the desire and the temptation.

Nothing was settled between them, nothing sure. She wouldn't give up her technology and he wouldn't give up his bid. She had been raised—for a few years, at least—by a woman like him, one who put wealth before all else. In turn, Erik had been hurt, and bore wounds on the outside and inside.

But it was those wounds that called to her. Maybe it was stupid, but now that she understood more of what had happened, more of what had made him into the man she'd come to know, his moods seemed less important, his gruffness a barrier rather than an assault.

She didn't know if she could trust him, or trust the feelings that swirled through her, stronger than she'd expected. Stronger than she wanted. But she couldn't ignore them any more than she could refuse to dive once the plane was in the sky. It wasn't in her nature.

When in doubt, she jumped.

She slid her hands up from his forearms to his chest, and lingered there a moment to feel the strong, steady beat of his heart, then up to link her fingers behind his neck and pull him all the way down for a kiss. A real one.

She softened her lips and opened her mouth, inviting him in, wordlessly telling him that it was okay, that this was right, that there was more than chemistry and enmity between them, though she couldn't have said what.

Then it was her turn to pause and wait for him to meet her halfway. She knew he had his own decisions to make—whether he trusted her enough to let down his guard, whether he would make the implicit promise in becoming lovers, that he would be willing to compromise on the NPT technology.

For a moment she worried that the pull between them wouldn't be enough. Then his lips firmed against hers, and there were no more questions.

His lips said, *Yes, I trust you this far.* His tongue touched hers, saying, *Yes, we can find a way to compromise, a way to make this work for both of us.* His arms, when they came up to band around her waist, pressing their bodies together with intimate contact, said, *Yes, this is right for me. I want this. I need this.*

Or maybe the want and need came from her. From both of them. It didn't seem to matter anymore when their tongues finally touched after what seemed far too long.

Meg slid into the kiss on a flare of heat and relief, and a tiny thread of something that felt like nerves, fear not of Erik but of the emotions that pounded in her chest and pressed at her throat and eyes until she felt wetness gather.

Don't make this into something it's not, she told herself as he held her closer, kissing her and touching her waist and hips through clothing that suddenly seemed like more hindrance than covering.

He pulled away far enough to say, "Bedroom. Upstairs."

She didn't tell him she'd already been up there, simply turned, looped an arm around his waist, and started walking.

They'd said everything that needed to be said. Now was the time for action.

Lots of action.

It wasn't until they were halfway up the wide, rubber-edged stairs that she realized he didn't have his cane. It must have fallen in the kitchen—she vaguely remembered hearing a clatter over the clamor of blood and heartbeat in her ears. He leaned on her slightly with each step, seeming not to care in his haste to gain the bedroom.

Then he glanced down at her and she realized he cared a great deal when he said, "Second thoughts?"

The shadows in his eyes suggested he might be

having second thoughts of his own, and he leaned more heavily with the next step, as though trying to emphasize the gimp. She thought about stepping away, about showing him he was less crippled than he perceived, and even if he wasn't, who the hell cared? It was just a leg, not the man.

But she knew damn well that would break the mood and leave things unfinished between them. They had been heading this way from the moment they'd met. So instead of making a point she could make another time, under other circumstances, she cocked her head and smiled. "My only second thought is whether we should wait for the bedroom, but I'm thinking the stairs would be uncomfortable."

"No argument there." He bent and kissed her, hard and hot, and quick enough that he was gone by the time she assembled herself to respond. Then he stepped away, took her hand and tugged her up the stairs, limping on his own two feet and not seeming to care that she saw.

They were hurrying by the time they hit the stairs, running by the time they reached the bedroom. He paused at the threshold, and she darted past him, afraid he would offer to carry her, afraid it would mean too much to her in a situation that couldn't mean everything.

This isn't a big deal, she told herself. It's just spaghetti and sex.

Then he was in the bedroom with her and it seemed like so much more than that.

He used the switch just inside the door to click off

the light, leaving only the hallway illumination. She would have protested that she wanted to see him, but knew he was going for more than ambience. He wanted the privacy of darkness.

She stopped beside the bed, and he paused a few feet from the door. The familiar tension crackled in the air between them, but warmer now, less desperate. They were coming together not in a moment of mindless passion—though passion simmered beneath the surface as her heart beat up into her throat—but in accord. She respected him, needed him, wanted him, even l—liked him, and hoped he felt the same for her.

Even knowing she'd skipped a vital word in her own thoughts, she lifted a hand and beckoned him closer. "Come on. We've got all night."

Chapter Twelve

Meg's words might have been brazen, but by the time Erik crossed the bedroom and stood in front of her, she'd worked up a major case of nerves.

It was a good bet she hadn't forgotten how to make love—it was like riding a bicycle and all that—but it had been a while for her, and longer since it had meant something. And, like it or not, this meant something.

"I don't, um, have anything." She gestured awkwardly. "You know, protection." *Real smooth, Doc. Way to be a new millennium girl.*

"I do." But his brows furrowed. "I think. Somewhere." He shot her a sidelong look and his lips twitched.

A giggle bubbled up her throat. She swallowed it, but the pressure emerged in an unladylike snort.

Then they were laughing together, a friendly, happy sound that dispelled the weirdness and made them feel like allies.

"I'll try the bathroom, you search the bedside

tables." Still snickering, he stumped to the master bath at the back corner of the bedroom and snapped on the light, adding more brightness to the bedroom. She heard him mutter, "Real smooth, Falco."

The parallel to her earlier thought made her laugh again, as a strange joy expanded within her, a sense of having found something precious and wonderful where she'd least expected it. She'd found a friend. A lover. A love.

Don't get ahead of yourself, she cautioned, but deep inside she knew it was already too late. Somehow, impossibly, she'd fallen for Erik Falco. She couldn't have said when it had happened, but the truth sparkled through her like free-falling through a rainbow.

Okay, you're already ahead of yourself. But for God's sake, don't tell him *about it.*

Her internal voice had a point there, she thought as she pulled out the top drawer of one bedside table and found spare change and a few rubber bands. As she shut the drawer, Erik's earlier words echoed in her head. *She made me meat loaf, told me she loved me and took me to bed.* Well, she'd already made him dinner and was fully intending to take him to bed. So she'd skip the declaration of love. He didn't need the weirdness factor, and they'd get around to the emotions later.

"Any luck?" he called from the bathroom, where she could hear the sounds of rummaging.

"Not yet." She moved to the other side of the bed. "These things aren't going to be mummified, are they? Condoms do have expiration dates."

That earned her another guffaw, a happy, masculine sound that lodged a bubble of joy beneath her heart.

"Seasoned, perhaps, but not mummified." He popped his head around the door frame, expression open, looking young and handsome, and so unlike the brooding, suspicious man she'd first met. "My older brother, Nev, and his girlfriend used a 'mummified' condom and wound up pregnant their sophomore year of college. Everything worked out okay—they're still married, three kids, dog, yadda yadda—but he beat it into Robbie and me that we had to change out our condom supply every six months without fail. January and June. Even if it was a new box, dump the supply and start over." He shrugged. "I've kept up the habit. Stupid, really. I can't tell you how many boxes I've chucked since the shooting."

The admission made her want to hold him, but she knew he would see the action as pity rather than sympathy, so she grinned instead. "Yet you don't know where they are." She pulled out the bedside table drawer. "Aha! Found 'em. Right behind the gun. Where else would they be?"

She told herself there was a joke in there, but suddenly couldn't find the humor as she stared down at the weapon, which was made of matte-black metal and showed worn patches on the molded plastic of the hand grip.

A strong arm reached past her and picked up the weapon, leaving the unopened, plastic-wrapped box of condoms untouched.

"It's loaded, since I'm the only one here and I know not to mess with it. Thirteen bullets for luck." He pointed to the bottom of the grip first, then to the side. "Clip goes here, safety here. It's on now. This is off." He slid a small button to reveal a red dot. "Point and shoot."

"I don't… I'm not…" She shivered. "Sorry. I was trying to find a joke there and I couldn't." The dark night outside the windows suddenly seemed closer than it had moments before, the danger not as far away as she would have liked.

He clicked the safety back on, returned the weapon to its drawer, and turned Meg to face him. His eyes were serious when he said, "It's probably best for you to know where it is and how to use it. I'll have the smaller 9 mm with me, but this was my service piece. It's here if you need it."

"I won't need it," she said quickly, then paused and said, "I don't *want* to need it. But if I do, I'll know where to look."

But they both knew that if anything happened, there wouldn't be time for her to look. So far, the attacks had been stealthy, and jarring in their unpredictability.

"Hey." He touched a finger beneath her chin, tipping her head up so she saw the truth in his eyes when he said, "I'm not going to let anything happen to you. I swear it. I don't know if this bastard is after you because of me, or whether you were the target all along. At this point I don't care. He'll have to come through me first."

The banked passion behind his words shimmered through her, resonating as though he'd promised to love her rather than keep her safe. She suspected the two were inextricably intertwined in his psyche.

Or maybe she needed to think they were.

Either way, she stepped close to him and tangled her fingers with his. "I trust you to protect me, but right now I need you to do something else." *I need you to love me,* she nearly said, but the words stuck in her throat.

He seemed to hear them anyway, because he reached up to frame her face, drawing their linked hands together so she was touching her own skin when he kissed her.

She murmured agreement and crowded close, welcoming the heat that drove away the chill of nerves and uncertainty. Where before there had been awkwardness, laughter or fear, now there was only the rush of blood and sensation.

Now there was only him.

She moaned as he feathered kisses along her jaw and down her throat, reawakening nerve endings that had gone too long unstimulated. When she loosened her hands from his and touched them flat to his chest, she could feel the heat of him through the soft cotton shirt, the layers of muscle and man over bone, and the quick, excited beat of his heart.

He touched her through her clothes, tracing her curves and telling her without words that she was sexy rather than solid, attractive rather than just athletic. A feminine warmth blossomed beneath his hands, making her feel delicate and vulnerable, yet powerful at the same time.

She rode the feeling of power and slid her hands down, then up again beneath his untucked shirt so she touched his bare skin. She reveled in his indrawn breath and the quick shudder of reaction. She skimmed her fingertips along his muscled ribs, scraping lightly with her nails, testing his reaction, testing her power.

He muttered an oath and quickly unbuttoned the shirt and cast it aside, leaving him bare from the waist up. She wished she could have seen him in more than the reflected light from the hallway and bath, but the dimness lent an intimacy to the scene, a hint of unintentional romance that shouldn't have mattered, but did.

Her heart pounded, sending heated blood radiating from her chest to her extremities with such force that her fingers and cheeks tingled with it.

She gloried in the rasp of sensation when he slid his hands beneath her shirt and teased the skin at her waist. *Higher,* she wanted to say. *More.* But his raspy chuckle as he retook her mouth told her that he knew exactly what she wanted, and was enjoying the torture. Enjoying the game.

Knowing two could play at that, and remembering having once been good at the push-pull of lust, she threw herself into the kiss, sliding her hands up along his bare chest to twine at his neck, binding the two of them together as they kissed long and deep and the world outside spun away.

It was like free-falling, only better because it went on and on and on, and there wasn't that critical moment when she had to pop her canopy free. The feelings just built and built until she thought she might explode, but she never hit the ground.

Just kept falling.

She felt the give of the mattress beneath her, the unyielding weight of man above, and reveled in the intimate press even as she resented the friction of her binding clothes. Naked. She wanted to be naked with him, around him.

They rolled across the king-size expanse, grappling not for dominance, but for pleasure. Giving it. Receiving it. The dimly lit darkness became a cocoon for soft sighs and groans, for whispers of discovery and delight, even for a moment or two of laughter, as the easy accord they'd unexpectedly discovered during the condom search spilled over into their lovemaking. She remembered the heat from her other experiences, but not the intensity. And certainly not the physical freedom she found when they shed the last of their clothes and the dimness bound them in quietly frenzied intimacy.

She didn't think of the faint sag from weight loss or the places where she was more strong than sexy, didn't think of anything other than Erik's body—the feel of his skin and muscle beneath her questing fingertips, the rasp of hair at his chest and tautly muscled stomach, the twine of their legs as they kissed and kissed again.

She slid her bare foot up his calf and felt the irregular ridges of scar tissue. He stiffened slightly against her, but she didn't back down, didn't move away, just kept up a slow stroke of toe against calf and the inciting glory of their kisses until he relaxed again and caught up with her, then raced ahead, skimming his hands up to cup her breasts. She couldn't think then, couldn't focus on anything but the quickening glide of his clever fingers and the intimate press of their bodies as the covers bunched up and over them, creating pockets of friction and heat countered by cool draughts feathering over their sweat-slicked bodies.

Outside it was the crisp chill of a New England fall night, but inside held the tropical steaminess of summer. Meg tasted the salt of exertion, of sex. Urgency built in her core and radiated outward, begging for completion, demanding it.

"Where was that box again?" she asked, and laughed when her voice cracked, then laughed again when Erik rolled across the bed to retrieve the condoms. He was glorious in his nakedness, limned in the yellow hallway light, which cast the ripples, hollows and juts of his masculine physique in sharp relief as he punched through the plastic wrapper, withdrew a foil packet and rolled the protective layer down over his proud erection.

The motion should have been more practical than erotic, but the light, the heat and the man combined to leave Meg dry-mouthed and salivating at the same time, churned up and aching to have that hard, driving flesh within her.

Instead of waiting for him to return, waiting for more of those deep, weightless kisses, she rolled to him, threw a leg over his waist and kissed him, all in one smooth move that left her straddling him, dizzy with desire and the spinning, swirling heat.

He muttered an oath and brought his hands up to grasp her hips. His fingertips dug deep and held on as she eased back and down, seating the tip of him inside her wet, wanting cleft.

In the darkness, she couldn't see the color of his eyes, couldn't tell if they darkened with anticipation and desire. But she could see the intensity that burned in their depths when his hands urged her to slide down along his sheathed length, inch by filling inch until he was seated to the hilt and she was suspended above him, borne on the thick-feeling air, the brace of her numb arms and the strength of his fingers as they dug into her hipbones.

And urged her to move.

She eased forward and then back, riding the surge of pleasure and the power that came when his eyes clouded and then closed. Her next move wrung a strangled groan from his throat and she wondered what the other pharma-tech corporate raiders would think if they knew that Erik Falco could be rendered wordless by the pleasure they created together.

Then she thought nothing at all, as her own half-formed wordlets were swept aside, caught up in the rising tide of heat and motion as the pace quickened between them.

The room spun and grew dark, startling her until

she realized her eyelids had drifted shut. No matter, the swirling sensations were enough, they were everything as the pleasure built to a peak within her.

The world tilted as Erik neatly reversed their positions so he was above her, thrusting into her with building fervor and iron control. He eased the weight off his injured leg, creating an exquisite angle of penetration, one that touched new nerve bundles within her, setting off a chain reaction of pleasure that quickly built to a conflagration.

She grabbed on to him, seeking an anchor as gravity spun out beneath her and the free fall accelerated. She called his name as he surged deeper and deeper still. The blood rushed in her ears, sounding like windsong, and the anticipation built to a fever pitch.

Then, when she thought she couldn't stand it, when she couldn't wait any longer for the final moment, sensation exploded within her, around her, inside her with a noise like the *boom* of an opening canopy.

Then she hung motionless. The free fall stopped. The windsong stopped. She hovered hundreds of feet above the earth, suspended only by the feel of the man around her. Inside her.

Pleasure radiated outward, holding her in place, holding her helpless to do anything but feel.

She felt Erik's arms tighten around her, felt him press his cheek to hers in a tender, binding gesture as he poured himself into her on one final, forceful surge. She felt his flesh pump within her, felt her inner muscles contract to hold him in place and prolong the flight.

Then slowly, ever so slowly, from one heartbeat to the next, they floated back to earth until she could feel the mattress at her back and the good, heavy weight of man at her front, where he had collapsed on top her in the aftermath.

She didn't want to turn her head to look at him, wasn't sure she wanted to know how much it had—or hadn't—meant to him. Deep in her soul, she knew it had meant far too much for her.

I love you, her inner voice whispered. Too soon, perhaps, but no less real for the speed of falling. Of impact.

But he wouldn't want to hear that. Not now. Maybe not for quite a while. She told herself she could wait, she could let this grow at its own speed, let them get past the hurdles still remaining for them—finding the attacker, working out the kinks in the licensing so they were both satisfied. Then she could use the words. But not now. Now was too soon.

So instead of pressing a kiss into the sweat-slicked hollow of his neck and saying *I love you,* she turned her head in the opposite direction, toward the bedside table and the square of light that shone from the bathroom, reflecting on the open box of condoms. "Oh, hell. You've only got a six-pack."

He chuckled, that rusty, unfamiliar sound that did a little dance beneath her heart. He snaked out an arm and snagged the box without looking. "Then we'll have to make the other five count."

Chapter Thirteen

The six-pack of condoms had a sole survivor by morning. Erik lay back happy and spent, with energy humming beneath his skin, even though his muscles were nearly limp with fatigue. He eyed the half-open door of the master bath and the shower steam curling around the edges, and briefly considered joining Meg in there with the last condom.

But something held him back. A need for a breath of space, perhaps, or a moment of lucidity without her soft skin a touch away, her softer lips in range.

He wanted to push her away as much as—if not more than—he wanted to join her. He'd never intended to let it go this far.

No, he admitted, that wasn't true. He'd been fascinated by her the moment she'd turned down his first few offers for the NPT technology, from the moment the investigator's file had landed on his desk and he'd learned that Dr. M. Corning was a strawberry-blond pain in the butt.

He'd wanted her for weeks. Months, even.

Wanted to have her. Touch her. Taste her. And now that he'd had the experience, his need for her was by no means slaked. If anything it was worse, because he knew what she tasted like, what she felt like underneath him, around him, how she moaned his name in the back of her throat when she came.

He knew all that now, and it made the wanting stronger.

Worse, it made him care for her more than was comfortable.

He shifted beneath the sheets as his blood heated again, as a few words filtered out from the shower and he learned something else about Dr. M. Corning.

She sang in the shower. Badly.

A faint smile touched his lips and a fainter thought entered his heart.

What if they could make this thing between them last? They were intelligent, mature adults. They could agree to disagree on the NPT deal, couldn't they? It was business, after all. He'd help Peters and Sturgeon get the bastard hunting her, they'd let the lawyers figure out the NPT deal, and then maybe they could take a few days away. Someplace pretty, where the leaves were just turning. Or maybe farther north, where the snows had already begun. He didn't ski anymore, but that wouldn't matter.

The past eight hours had shown him he still had plenty of leg left for other, more important activities.

He grinned at the memory of those activities, and felt the grin widen when Meg emerged from the steamy bathroom, wearing a towel and a smile of her own.

"Hey, sleepyhead." She crossed the room to an upholstered chair. He'd never thought about the decor much when he'd escaped the city and stayed at the house, but now, watching her bend over the chair to collect her discarded clothing, watching the towel ride up over her long, taut thigh, he decided he freaking loved that chair. Maybe he'd even buy another, just to watch her bend over it. Then he could—

"I can feel you staring, Falco." But she looked over her shoulder, arched a brow and waggled her butt, letting him know she didn't mind one bit.

"Yeah, well, I like the scenery." Erik folded his hands behind his head on the pillow and grinned. "Don't let me distract you. Unless you'd like to be distracted?"

She grinned as she stepped into her panties, pulling them up beneath the towel. "You've had your distractions, buster. We've got work to do."

That had him sitting up in the wide bed. "What work? You're safe here."

She shimmied into her bra and buttoned the white shirt over it before she jerked her chin at the window, where gauzy drapes framed a clear blue sky dotted with puffy, perfect clouds. "You said you'd moved the sale up to today, right? I'd fight you, but I haven't been able to get the licensing deal done and I'm out of options, so why bother? Besides, things are different now." She smiled at him. "We'll need to meet with Cage and the lawyers at Boston General and get the new paperwork drawn up."

A deadly chill chased through Erik's bloodstream. "What new paperwork?"

She pulled on her pants, hopping on one foot so her back was to him when she said, "Why, making sure we agree on the scope of the sale, of course." She straightened and turned to him. "It's not like you're going to insist on an outright sale now that we're together." When he said nothing, her shoulders tightened beneath the white shirt. "Are you?"

Erik stayed frozen in place, flesh cold beneath the sheet that provided scant barrier between him and the realization that he'd done it again.

He'd fallen for a woman who wanted something from him.

"Erik?" Her voice sounded small and quavery, and though part of him wanted to believe it was an act, the more self-aware portion of him knew it was genuine—and therefore a bigger problem—when she said, "You're not actually going to force the deal now, are you? I thought we had an understanding."

He rubbed his chest, where a low, aching weight had settled beneath a sluggish stir of anger. "So did I, but I'm starting to think we weren't understanding the same thing. I thought we would keep this—" he gestured between the two of them "—separate from the business dealings. That we could be professionals and lovers at the same time."

Something flashed in her eyes, seeming caught between hurt and anger. "Spoken like a true businessman. Can you really shut it off that easily? Is your heart really that hard?" She took a step back, into a square of light framed by the gossamer drapes. "I thought we could compromise. Work together."

Pressure built from the back of his head to the front, a relentless vise of frustration and anger, directed equally at himself and the woman standing opposite him, watching him with dark, wounded eyes. "There is no compromise, Meg. I want all of the technology, not a relatively unimportant part of it."

Pure anger flashed in her eyes this time, and her breath hissed out between her teeth. "*Relatively unimportant?* NPT is going to be a godsend for women everywhere. No more Byzantine needles poking into their stomachs, sucking up amnio fluid or scraping off a few CV cells. No more spontaneous abortions when the needle doesn't go in quite right. No more infections or—" She stopped and gritted her teeth. "A *businessman* should be able to see the huge potential for profit."

Erik swung his legs off the mattress, keeping the sheet over them on a burst of the modesty he'd lost during the night. His pulse pounded with the need for action, for a fight, but who would he fight? The mistake, it appeared, had been his. He'd deluded himself into believing in something that didn't exist between them.

"I see the potential just fine," he said between gritted teeth. "However, the prenatal testing aspects aren't why I tendered my offer. I'm looking at this from another direction." He reached down to his injured calf and dug a thumb into the tight muscle, trying to relieve the pressure of overuse and stress.

Her eyes followed the motion and an awful sort of comprehension flickered to life. She swallowed. "You want to develop the fetal cells as progenitors, don't you?"

She made it sound as if he'd just suggested frying a puppy for breakfast.

"Why not?" he demanded. "I'm sure you've read the studies. Those very fetal cells you've found cruising around in the mother's bloodstream have been known to migrate to the site of an injury and help with healing. They're pluripotent—they can grow into any kind of cell type, fix any kind of injury."

He rose and pulled the sheet around his body toga-style so he could look down at her and gesture at the world outside. "Think about it. With proper development, we might be able to harvest those cells from a mother and use them to fix her paralyzed child's spinal injury. Better yet, since half of the child's DNA comes from each parent, those cells could be used to heal either the mother or the father. Another sibling, perhaps. Just think of the possibilities!"

She took a step back, eyes wide in her face. "I *have* thought of the possibilities, Erik. That's the problem. You see a way to fix yourself. I see an ethical issue right up there with fetal experimentation."

Knowing those were fighting words, Erik headed to his walk-in closet and grabbed trousers, a shirt and tie, needing the barrier of business clothing. From inside the echoing space, he said, "You're being overly dramatic. I'm not talking about combining an egg and sperm, growing it to the sixteen-cell stage in some lab and then performing experiments, on the theory that it's not a 'person' yet. I'm talking about filtering cells out of a mother's bloodstream and using them to help her, or to help another member of her family."

"Precisely." There was an unfamiliar chill in her voice when she said, "But what if there isn't a child? Take you, for example. It's unlikely your mother's bloodstream would still carry your cells after all this time. So what are you going to do, marry someone just to have your child? Pay them? And then once the baby's cells have been isolated from her blood, what then? Abort the child because you have what you need? Let the mother carry it to term and raise the baby, knowing it's only alive because you needed a few cells to fix your limp?"

Something iced in his chest. He emerged from the closet with his slacks hooked over his hips and his chest bare, a starched shirt in his hand. "That's not fair. You want to talk about what else isn't fair? It's not right that a high school kid can break his neck playing hockey and never walk again. Not when there's a way we could help fix him."

"Help fix *you,* you mean." There was pity in her expression, and it made him mean.

"Yes, damn it. I want to be fixed. I want to walk without a damned cane. I want to ski again. Jog again. Hell, just get up the damned stairs without leaning on something. I've got the money—why can't I have the technology?"

Her lips firmed. "Because it's not right and you know it."

He turned his back on her, gimped back into the closet and reached for socks. "I know nothing of the sort. And if you think one night of sex is enough to buy me off, think again."

He braced himself for her burn of anger, for the curses that were sure to come, the curses he'd surely earned.

But they didn't come. She was silent for a long moment. Too long.

"What, no comeback for that?" He kept the words rough and angry, but inside he already knew what he would find when he stepped back inside the bedroom.

Sure enough, she was already gone.

MEG TOOK ERIK'S GUN from the bedside table, and when she called a cab from the downstairs phone, she had the driver meet her by the front steps.

She was furious, but she wasn't stupid.

She half expected Erik to come crashing down the stairs to continue their fight. The fact that he didn't only confirmed what their conversation had taught her. She'd been deluding herself when she'd thought they were on the same page.

Hell, they weren't even reading the same book.

"Better to figure it out now versus later," she told herself, and tried to believe in the words. But tears scratched at the back of her throat. She held herself tense, half hoping he'd come down the stairs, half hoping he wouldn't.

He hadn't appeared by the time the cab pulled up.

"Your loss," she muttered as she punched in the codes that would let her out of the house, out of the place where she'd thought for a few hours that she might have found something special.

"My mistake," she said, and slammed the door.

She didn't look back as she climbed in the cab and gave the hospital's address.

The driver's eyes flashed with surprise. "You sure, lady? That's all the way in the city. It'll take forever with rush-hour traffic."

"You got somewhere else to be?" She stared through the windshield, refusing to look at the house, refusing to care whether he was watching or not. "I've got the money if you've got the time."

"You're the boss." The driver pulled away from the house. As they turned onto the main road and headed for the highway, a police cruiser fell in behind them.

The cabbie eased his foot off the accelerator and shifted into the slow lane, but the cop car didn't pass. It stayed a comfortable few lengths back, just waiting. Watching.

Well, that answered it, Meg thought on a beat of depression, a press of tears. Erik knew she'd gone. He'd leaned on Peters or the local cops to have her followed, but he hadn't come downstairs, hadn't asked her to stay.

Either he didn't care nearly as much as she did or he figured that it was hopeless. That *they* were hopeless.

She was good and angry by the time they hit the highway. How could he have made love to her knowing he had no intention of compromising on the NPT sale? Worse, she thought with a clutch of disgust, he wanted to develop the exact thing she'd been fighting to block all this time.

Yes, the fetal stem cells could be used to help patients, but at what cost to society?

A blip of siren from behind yanked her attention back to the road. The cabbie cursed and flipped on his blinker before easing to the side of the road. "I wasn't doing anything, you—"

"It's me," Meg said. "It's okay, though. Just see what they have to say."

The cruiser rolled up beside the cab and the passenger window buzzed down. The cabbie's window was already at half-mast, so the cop's words carried over the background traffic noise when he said, "Dr. Corning? We'll need you to follow us."

Her blood chilled. "What? What's happened?"

"I can't say, ma'am, but Mr. Falco said—and I quote—'Tell her to turn her bleeping phone on.'"

"Oh, hell." Meg reached for her purse and rummaged for her phone, knowing Erik likely hadn't used the word "bleeping" at all.

Worry beat at her. What had happened? Something with Raine? Something with the lab? Another attack? What?

Her phone was dead. "My battery's out," she

called, but it was too late. The cruiser window was up, and the car was bulling its way into the thickening traffic, lights flashing.

"Are you in trouble, lady?" The driver's eyes met hers in the mirror, reflecting his real question. *Am I in trouble?*

"Just follow him," she said, not really answering either question. "We'll be going to Boston General."

That was where it had all begun, after all.

WHEN HE HIT the second traffic snarl, Erik banged his steering wheel and cursed with impotent frustration.

How had everything fallen apart so quickly? Just the day before, they'd been on the right track. Meg had been safe and they'd been successfully fighting the attraction between them. The detectives had been working to find the young man from the hospital video. They hadn't had a name or a connection to one of his competitor companies, but they'd had a face, damn it. Things had been starting to move.

Now those same things were starting to crumble. Raine had taken a turn for the worse—the doctors had been cagey about it on the phone because he wasn't an actual blood relative and Meg hadn't been there to pull rank. She was ahead of him somewhere, with the cops escorting her to Boston General.

Maybe it was better that way, better to have her protected by men who hadn't woken up beside her, who hadn't brought tears to her eyes.

He'd thought they understood each other, but they

hadn't understood anything. As he drove, a lead weight settled on Erik's chest, right above his heart.

He hadn't meant to hurt Meg, hadn't meant to care for her. In the end, he'd done both of those things. There was nothing he could do to fix the hurt—he needed the NPT technology, believed it was the answer he'd been seeking. He hadn't meant to be cruel, though, and feared that was exactly what he'd done.

"Come on, come on!" He cursed the traffic and leaned on his horn, as if that would do anything to shift the lumbering bus ahead of him.

He told himself Meg would be fine with the cops. They'd keep her safe until he got there.

But deep down inside, he wasn't sure.

MEG'S POLICE ESCORT directed her to the critical care floor, warning her that something had happened with Raine. When she met Max coming the other way and saw the bleak desperation in his normally contained expression, she feared the worst.

"What happened?" When he plowed past, seeming not to see or hear her, she grabbed his arm. "Max, what's wrong? Is Raine…?"

He blinked and shook his head before focusing on her. His eyes cleared a notch, letting her see the unhappiness. "She lost the baby. She got up in the middle of the night and fell. Said she saw a shadow, but the guard was at his post and there was nobody in the room. There was so much blood…" He looked away, unhappiness etched in the tight muscles of his neck and jaw.

"I'm sorry." She tightened her fingers on his arm. "If you want to stay with her, I can—"

"She kicked me out." He stepped away from Meg's touch. "And don't tell me it was just hormones, or reaction, or whatnot. I know all that. But I saw her eyes. She's not interested. No, scratch that—she's decided not to be interested. There's a difference."

Meg thought back to her morning with Erik. "Yeah. I know what you mean."

"Jemma called," he said, changing the subject. "She asked me to meet her in the lab—something to do with the Phase IV data. She sounded kind of funny on the phone, but she wouldn't give me any specifics."

Oh, great, Meg thought, that was just what she didn't need. A problem with the NPT clinical trials would ruin any chance of persuading Cage to kill the deal with FalcoTechno.

Not that she had much hope to begin with.

Face it, she was pretty much out of luck.

Meg muttered an oath, took another look at Max's face and made a quick decision. "You take a walk. I'll head upstairs and deal with Jemma."

He nodded distractedly. "You'll be okay? Where's Falco?"

"He's on his way," she answered, bending the truth just a little. No doubt he'd be here soon. He'd go straight to Raine's room to check on her, and Meg would rather not be there to meet him.

She'd be safe enough heading upstairs. Jemma was already there, and hell, she was carrying an illegal concealed weapon, which weighed heavily in the pocket of her green blazer. She'd be fine.

And if she kept repeating that, maybe she'd start to believe it. But Raine's nightmare—or had it been something more?—along with the pall that seemed to permeate the hospital air, denser and more desperate than usual, had her tensing.

Max exhaled. "Okay. I could use some air." He strode toward the nearest exit, a big, strong man who'd had the legs knocked out from underneath him by a woman he'd met less than a week earlier.

Yeah. She knew how that felt.

Meg grimaced and turned toward the elevators. She stiffened when a figure rounded the corner, a twentysomething guy in low-slung jeans and a dark hooded sweatshirt. What she could see of his face looked sullen and petulant, and he walked with a loose, aggressive stride.

He looked an awful lot like the guy in the fax.

She slid her hand into her jacket pocket, felt the warm weight of Erik's gun slip into her palm, felt the nub of the safety beneath her fingertip, and—

The guy's face cleared and broke into a smile. "There you are!" He sped up, jogged past Meg, and embraced a young woman with an eyebrow ring, heavily made-up eyes and a hospital ID.

Meg winced. Hell. She'd nearly pulled a weapon on the gift shop attendant's boyfriend.

"Get a grip," she muttered, earning herself a scowl

from both halves of the cuddling couple. She waved them off. "Not talking to you. Carry on."

She felt foolish as she waited for the elevator, which was free now of its crime scene tape. Foolish and scared and unhappy, a far cry from the almost-in-control-of-her-life-and-headed-in-the-right-direction delusions she'd been harboring just a week earlier.

How had she lost control of things so quickly? More importantly, how could she regain that control and reassert herself against an opponent who had far more money and power than she did?

An idea flickered as the elevator doors slid open, then was gone when she realized it was the same elevator that had fallen with her and Erik in it.

She opted for the stairs instead, and felt the gun bang against her hip with each stride.

By the time she reached the fifth-floor landing, she had the bare bones of a plan, a last-ditch effort to convince—and if necessary force—Cage to turn down FalcoTechno's offer.

She didn't want to do it, but she didn't see any other choice.

Running the details in her mind, she pushed open the door to the main lab. "Jemma? It's me. Max said you were having a problem up here?"

The young woman's voice responded from the inner lab, garbled by walls and distance.

Meg didn't bother ditching her blazer and pulling on a lab coat. She headed straight into the lab, shouldering through the heavily shielded door. "So I was thinking," she began, and stepped into the lab. "What if we—"

A heavy blow caught her from behind, driving her to her knees.

And everything faded to black.

Chapter Fourteen

Erik dumped his car in the Emergency entrance, knowing it would be towed and not caring in the least. He bolted to the front door, moving as fast as his leg would let him.

He'd finally gotten through to a doctor who'd talk to him, but the news wasn't good. Raine had lost the baby. The knowledge was a painful pressure in his chest. What if he'd been there? What if he'd stayed with Raine rather than gone home to Meg?

Raine might not have fallen, and he and Meg wouldn't have spent the night together, wouldn't have made the mistake of thinking they understood each other.

Muttering, Erik limped past a solitary figure leaning against the hospital wall. Then he stopped. Turned back. "Max? What are you doing out here? Why aren't you inside with Raine and Meg?"

He hadn't been able to reach Meg on her cell

phone, but told himself it didn't matter. The cops had followed her in. The rent-a-guard was watching Raine's room. The women were safe.

"Raine kicked me out." Something dark and dangerous moved in the big man's eyes—jealousy, maybe, and something more. Something hurting and sad. "You should talk to her."

"I will. Later." He knew he owed her an apology, an explanation. But he owed Meg one first. "Where's Meg?"

Max jerked his chin upward. "She's in the lab with Jemma."

When the hospital doors opened and a familiar figure stepped out carrying a cup of takeout coffee, Erik's blood froze in his veins. "No, she's not." He raised his voice. "Jemma, where's Meg?"

The young woman's expression darkened when she saw the men, saw their worried expressions. "I thought she was with you."

"No," Max said quickly. "I told you she was on her way in. And besides, why aren't you in the lab?"

Jemma frowned, confused. "Why would I be? And what do you mean, you told me? I haven't talked to you since yesterday."

Erik had his phone out and was speed-dialing Detective Peters before she'd finished speaking. "Damn it. We've been played." When Peters picked up, he snapped, "Get over here. Meg's upstairs with the guy."

"I'm on my way," the detective said, voice rushed. "Our techs got a hit on the face."

Hot rage cracked through the ice around Erik's heart. "You know who he is?"

"Not he. She."

CONSCIOUSNESS RETURNED with a rush of fear and disorientation. Meg groaned before she remembered what had happened, then bit off the noise to avoid detection.

Too late. Her captor had noticed she was awake.

A blurry shadow passed in front of her, a young man in low-slung jeans and a dark hooded sweatshirt.

Panic jammed her breath in her lungs. Oh, God. This was it. This was the man who'd been hunting her.

She tried to run, tried to spin away and escape, only to find her arms and legs bound. She was sitting on something with her hands fastened behind her back, her feet tied with her knees bent. As her brain began to clear with full consciousness she realized she was secured to one of the rolling lab chairs.

When the shadow passed again, Meg croaked, "Why?"

The young man sneered—only as the last of the cobwebs vanished, she realized it wasn't a young man at all. It was a woman sporting boys' clothing and a loose-limbed, masculine slouch. The woman's features rearranged themselves into a familiar pattern that made absolutely no sense until she said, "Because you can't have what I deserve."

Then she raised a weapon—Erik's service revolver, stolen from Meg's jacket—and took aim between Meg's eyes.

ERIK POUNDED up the stairs, cane gripped tightly in his hand, more weapon than crutch now. *Stay outside until we get there,* Peters had said. *She could be dangerous. Hell, she is dangerous.* But the cop's voice had echoed Erik's disbelief.

They'd been looking in the wrong direction all along. It had never been about FalcoTechno. It had been about Meg all along.

About professional jealousy.

He reached the fifth-floor landing and paused to assemble a mental map of the floor before he keyed in Meg's code—he'd memorized it over her shoulder on day one, just in case—and opened the door to the lab lobby.

Pulse loud in his head, he pressed his ear to the crack and listened, senses humming. Nothing.

The cops were on their way—he'd sent Max to stand extra guard on Raine, and told Jemma to wait for the detectives, who were ten, maybe fifteen minutes away through traffic. He should wait for backup. It was police protocol.

Hell, it was smart thinking.

He started to ease back, telling himself he didn't know the situation, wasn't a cop anymore. If his years on the force had taught him anything, it was that minutes counted in both directions. Moving too early was just as dangerous as too late. Perhaps more so.

For the first time in a long, long while, a fragment of memory came to him, a snippet in Jimmy's voice. "Steady, partner. You'll know when it's time."

And he always had, until that last day when he hadn't, when he'd gone in too soon and Jimmy had died.

"Come on, Peters. Where are you?" Erik pressed his ear to the crack once again, partly reassured by the quiet, partly fearing what it might mean.

Then he heard a voice. Voices. First Meg's, saying something low and groggy and trailing up at the end in an unintelligible question. Then the response from a woman he'd met only once before, one who hadn't even been on their radar screen as a suspect.

"Don't be stupid," the woman's voice said, faint with distance. "You and I both know there's only three ways for a female to get ahead in this field. She's born with connections, she sleeps her way to the top or she fights for it. You were born your father's daughter. Now that Leo Gabney's gone, I'm left with option three. Fight."

Not liking the woman's borderline manic tone, Erik damned his backup for being slow, eased the door open farther and slipped inside the deserted reception area. He eased his gun free as he worked his way across the open space and crouched behind Jemma's desk.

He heard movement in the lab, risked a look and saw that the main door, which was normally sealed, had been propped open with a chair.

Invitation, trap or something else? He didn't know and wasn't sure he could afford to find out.

Footsteps sounded within the lab and a shadow passed by the glass window of the propped-open door as a woman climbed on the chair and fiddled with something above the door.

Erik ducked down behind the desk and angled his head around the far side in the shadows, trying to see without being seen.

The shadow shifted and the woman poked her head through the partly opened door. She was wearing a young man's clothes and stance, but the hood of the sweatshirt was thrown back, revealing a face that was older and narrower than it should have been, pinched with tension and the mad fire that burned in eyes that were a lighter shade of brown than her brunette hair.

Annette Foulke, vice chair of the chemistry department.

They'd been so busy looking for the money angle, they'd overlooked the other major motivating force for crime.

Power.

"I know you're out there," she said. She didn't focus on the desk, though. Instead she addressed the lobby at large, including the open office doors in her sweeping statement. "I know you're listening, that you're scrambling to figure it out. But what's to figure? You want her. I have her." She smiled now, a cold twist of lips that wasn't quite sane. "I'm done being subtle. You couldn't figure it out on your own?

Well, let me help you. I want what's coming to me, or she dies. You've got five minutes."

She disappeared back through the doorway and pulled the chair away, letting the door shut and seal in her wake. That left Erik with almost nothing to go on besides two critical pieces of information. One, Annette Foulke had gone over the edge. Two, she had Meg.

They were looking at a hostage situation, damn it.

He swore under his breath, and grimaced when he realized his leg had cramped from the awkward position. He crab-walked around the desk, staying low, and opened the various drawers of Jemma's desk.

He hit paydirt on drawer three with the discovery of a small compact mirror. It was no more than two inches across, but it would have to do.

Breathing shallowly through his mouth, he eased away from the desk, toward the closed door. He was hoping for a crack, a gap beneath the panel that would let him get the mirror through, let him get a look at the situation. But that was a no-go. The lab door formed a tight seal around all four edges. No gaps. No cracks.

It made sense, he supposed. They would need to be able to seal off the lab space in case of a problem with radioactivity or chemicals. But that left him with too few options, too many questions.

He heard the rise and fall of Foulke's voice, heard the crash of something falling, and felt a jolt of adrenaline, the fear of being too early or too late. Weighing his options, he decided to risk it. He eased the mirror up the solid half of the door, to where the window began, and angled it so he could see a small slice of the lab beyond.

A clatter from the far side drew his attention. He tilted the mirror and saw Annette kick a piece of lab equipment, saw the expensive machine list to one side.

She was losing it. She was close to boiling over, and she'd put them on a deadline. Five minutes.

But five minutes for what? *Until* what?

He reversed the angle of the mirror and scanned the rest of the lab, almost afraid to see— There. He had her.

Meg's reflection shook until he steadied his hand through force of will. He squinted to make out details, and saw that she sat on a rolling chair with her hands behind her back and her feet bound in place. She was positioned between two of the large picture windows that ringed the lab, and seemed unhurt.

As he watched, she turned her head toward him— or rather toward the door and its stealthy mirror— and gestured with her head.

Fierce relief ran through him. She was okay. She knew he was here. Or rather, she knew someone was here. After their fight, he doubted she'd be too happy to learn it was him holding the mirror.

The thought brought an anxious twist. So many things to fix. Maybe not enough time.

He wanted to signal her, but he didn't dare. A quick turn of the reflection showed him that Annette was still occupied killing the piece of lab equipment.

But for how much longer? He couldn't be sure, but felt the seconds tick away.

He returned his attention to Meg while his mind spun. When she gestured a second time, jerking her chin upward, he followed the motion.

At first he didn't see it.

Then he did.

Terror sliced through him. She was positioned directly beneath the emergency shower, a spray head connected to the water main, designed as a first line of response in case of a chemical spill. If a lab worker was accidentally splashed with a toxic chemical, the emergency response protocol dictated that they jump under the shower and yank the handle, which would trip an alarm at the same time it released a gush of water.

Only this shower wasn't connected to the water main anymore. Even in the small mirror, Erik could see that the line had been interrupted. Now it led to three interconnected jugs of liquid, all fitted to what looked like a high-pressure pump.

It was a good bet those jugs didn't contain anything as benign as water.

Acid, his mind supplied on an adrenaline rush of horror. *Or a strong base.* It didn't matter which—both ends of the pH spectrum were equally dangerous, equally capable of melting flesh off bone on contact.

"Ssst!"

Erik whipped his head around at the hiss, tensing to duck and run while he got off a few shots of covering fire.

Through the half-open lab door, he saw Detective Peters hold a finger to his lips, signaling quiet.

Backup had arrived.

A muffled voice yanked Erik's attention back to the mirror. In an instant, his blood iced. Foulke's body blocked the reflected image. Her silhouette approached the door. The crank handle turned. The door eased open.

He slipped the safety on his weapon, going stone-cold at the knowledge that he would have only one chance.

Then he heard Meg's voice say, "Getting paranoid, Annette? Afraid they'll come for you? Afraid they'll get around the explosives you've set on the doors? Or are you afraid they *won't* come for you?"

The door slammed shut, muffling Annette's angry words.

Erik stifled the urge to yank open the door, roll in low and start firing. Too early. He had no plan. Too late. Annette had the doors wired somehow, apparently on a trip system that let her open from her side, but would blow if he opened it from his.

Like the other traps, it was clever and crude at the same time, and almost indefensible.

Almost.

Though it nearly killed him to do so, he pocketed the mirror and eased away from the door. He crossed the lobby, staying low and moving fast, and didn't let out a breath until he was back in the stairwell. The small space was crowded with bodies in bulletproof vests. Detectives Sturgeon and Peters were there, along with a handful of other cops wearing protective gear and guns. Jemma crouched at the edge of the group, lips pressed in a determined line. When she met Erik's eyes, she said, "I know the lab. I know how to get you in the back."

Erik shook his head. "She's booby-trapped the front and back doors of the main room." He quickly sketched the situation, trying to keep the emotion out of a voice that cracked on the strain. But the images were there in his brain—Jimmy's blood-soaked body sprawled on the road outside a corner bank, Meg's face when he'd told her of his plans for the NPT technology, the defiant timbre of her voice when she'd warned him of the trap.

The soft curve of her cheek and shoulder in the dimness as they'd made love the night before.

He traded a look with the head of the SWAT team, cop-to-cop. "Okay. Here's what we're going to do."

ANNETTE'S BREATH was sour on Meg's face when the older woman leaned close. Her hair was stringy and unkempt, but her clothes were laundered and smelled of fabric softener. The effect was jarring and just *wrong*.

"You think you're so smart," Annette hissed in a wash of poor hygiene so different from the hardworking, focused researcher she'd always seemed. "You think just because you're Robert Corning's daughter that you're untouchable. Well, you're not!" She jabbed a honed fingernail into Meg's shoulder, bringing a stabbing pain sharper than the ringing in her head or the dull ache of her bound joints.

"What does this have to do with my father?" Meg demanded, wanting to keep Annette talking past her arbitrary five-minute deadline. "I moved out when I was eighteen."

"You have his name," Annette said flatly. "He was a Nobel Prize winner, for God's sake. All your success trickles down from him. Men make the world go around. Women live in their shadows." She gestured to her outfit. "You see, Mother was right. Edward was always better than me. If I dress like him, *become* him, I can go places and do things a woman can't."

Meg shook her aching head and felt confused, desperate tears press. It was all too much—the buckets looming overhead, a noxious pairing of hydrochloric acid and sodium hydroxide, the mirror she thought she'd seen in the doorway, the crude devices wired to the only two exits…

Keep her talking, her sense of self-preservation insisted. *If she's talking, she's not doing—whatever she's going to do.*

Meg sucked in a breath. She thought she might have cracked a rib, but didn't know when, and tugged at her bonds, which had no give. "Who is—"

The lab intercom buzzed live, making both women jump. Then a male voice said, "Dr. Foulke. We'd like to talk to you."

For a wild, wishful moment, Meg thought the

voice belonged to Erik, just as she'd imagined he had been holding the small mirror in the doorway. But it didn't.

"This is Reid Peters of the Chinatown station," the detective's voice continued. "I've been authorized to ask for your demands and act on them, but only if we have proof that Dr. Corning is alive and well."

That earned her a glare from Annette. "You've got an *intercom?* Bitch." She leaned over Meg's main lab bench, puzzled over the phone for a few seconds, then stabbed the appropriate button. "She's alive, but I'm not talking to you. Get Zachary Cage. And make it fast."

Without waiting for an answer, she used a nearby rolling chair to climb up onto the lab bench, as she had when she'd first rigged the buckets to the emergency shower. Now, she pulled an old-fashioned kitchen egg timer from the pocket of her overlarge sweatshirt, cranked the timer to the halfway point, and attached it to the contraption overhead.

Then she returned to the phone. "You've got five minutes or the bitch is dead. And this time I mean it."

Meg heard the ticking overhead and started to count the seconds. She imagined the chaos outside her lab, cops and lab workers waiting to see what would happen next, or planning something desperate and futile that would never work.

There was no real way in or out of the lab except the doors. And the windows, of course, but they were five stories up and the radiation safety geeks made sure the sashes were kept locked. The vents were all self-contained and shielded, in case of a leak. Annette had inadvertently trapped her in one of the most secure locations on the hospital property.

Or, Meg thought, looking upward, maybe it wasn't an accident. Annette had been a step ahead of them all along. She had probably planned this.

But what was her goal? What did she want?

There was no answer as Annette stood in the center of the room, off by the automatic DNA sequencer she'd wrecked in a fit of rage minutes earlier. Her stillness and the contrast from the earlier violence was frightening.

The seconds built to minutes. A single drop of liquid fell from above and landed on the granite lab bench near Meg. There was no bubbling hiss of reaction—the benches were impervious to most chemicals—but she knew what would happen to human flesh. Burning. Pain.

Liquefaction.

She shuddered and tugged at her bonds again. They felt like rope, or maybe torn fabric. Another drop fell. Then another. The clock ticked down and an ominous whirring sound began to build overhead as the strange-looking mechanism attached to the shower began to activate.

Panic surged, overriding fear. Meg looked over and saw that Annette was still frozen in place, lips moving, attention turned inward.

Knowing this might be her only chance, Meg used her bound feet and weight to turn the chair around and scoot back against the lab bench. She raised her wrists and pressed them to the table.

And felt the burn when the first drop of acid landed.

ERIK LISTENED to the terse reports filtering into his earpiece, and gritted his teeth. He was balanced on a narrow cement ledge, five stories up, edging his way to a lab window Max swore he'd left open that morning, when Jemma's dust allergies had overridden the radiation geeks' strictures.

"Who's dumb idea was this again?" he muttered, knowing damn well it'd been his.

Detective Peters's voice crackled in his ear. "You say something, Falco?"

"I said I'm almost to the corner." He risked a look down and really wished he hadn't. The cars below were too far away, the air too empty.

He wasn't much higher than he'd been with Luke Cannon the day before—with one glaring difference. Well, three if he counted the lack of ropes, padding or belay buddy separately. It all added up to something he didn't want to deal with.

Yet he was dealing. For Meg.

He pressed his face to the rough wall and slid his right foot, testing for the next solid foothold. *Check and recheck your purchase,* Cannon's voice said in his head. *It's not that you shouldn't trust your bad leg—but you should proceed with caution.*

Only there wasn't time for caution, wasn't time to be weak or broken. With his cane tucked in his belt alongside his weapon, more talisman than crutch, he needed to rely on himself, and on the climbing skills he'd grossly exaggerated to Peters.

No sweat, he'd told the detective, *I could walk that in my sleep.* Only now he was sweating bullets as he reached the corner, where the narrow ledge fell away, only to reappear on the other side of the building. After that, it was just a few feet to the window that was supposedly open.

He swallowed, trying to find a hint of moisture in his too-dry mouth. "Any progress inside?"

"Cage is working on her now. Foulke keeps talking about someone named Edward, and how she should have had Meg's lab, should've had tenure, should've had a ton of things Meg got because of her father's name."

"You're kidding." Erik stopped dead on the realization that for all Meg's lectures about the purity of academia and the evils of industry, the danger had come from one of her own co-workers, over something as small—or as large—as tenure.

Then he resumed his progress. He slung his leg around the corner, closed his eyes, trusted his bad leg to hold, and stepped around.

He made it.

After what seemed like an hour, but was truly no more than a few seconds, he asked, "Time?"

"Ninety seconds left."

He nodded, though nobody could see him except a passing seagull and perhaps the odd pedestrian who might happen to look up the hospital wall. "I'm on it. Just a few more—"

"Hold it," Peters's voice interrupted. "There's something going on inside. There's—"

The window beside him exploded outward. A gun sounded once. Twice. Meg screamed.

Every fiber of Erik's being howled for him to dive through that window and come up firing, snapping off shot after shot to save the woman he lo— Yes, damn it, the woman he loved.

It didn't make any sense, but he loved her. He wanted her. He wanted to make it work with her, even though things seemed unworkable.

But he'd gone in too fast once before, with fatal consequences. He'd made every other mistake in the book with Meg, but he wouldn't make this one.

"Stand down," he said, trusting the earpiece to capture his words. "Don't go through those doors. I've got it."

And this time he wouldn't fail.

Chapter Fifteen

The second shot plowed into the heavy composite frame beneath the granite bench. Meg clamped her lips together, refusing to scream again and help Annette aim.

She'd overbalanced the chair to get out of the way of the first bullet when Annette had spun and fired without warning. Now she tugged furiously at her raw, burning wrists.

"Come on, *come on!*"

Tears of pain and fear blurred her vision as the buzzing from above grew louder and the noxious chemicals dripped faster, burning where they hit flesh.

Another few seconds and the shower would let go, dumping gallons of caustic chemicals onto her.

"Come on, you bastard!" She wasn't sure if she was cursing the woman standing in the center of the room, shifting sporadically between male and female personas, the bonds or the man she'd hoped would rescue her, but one last vicious tug brought a slice of pain, a rip of cloth and blessed release.

Her hands were free.

"Dr. Foulke? Annette? I'm here." Zachary Cage's voice spoke over the intercom, calm and placating, as though they were talking about vacation time rather than murder. "You said you wanted to talk to me, so let's talk."

"It's too late," Annette said to the room at large, her voice sliding into a lower, manly register. "You had your chance to promote me, to recognize everything I've done for you. Mother was—" Her voice caught, then steadied. "Mother was right. Sometimes a man has to *make* others see his value. That's what I'm doing. Making you see."

Meg could tell from the change in tone that Annette had turned toward her lab bench. She imagined the woman raising Erik's service revolver, imagined her aiming the weapon, tightening her finger on the trigger. Panic flared. Meg fumbled with the bonds securing her ankles to the chair. Her fingers cramped with pain as the acid continued to eat at flesh and tendon. She hadn't looked at the damage, hadn't been able to bear to look. The pain spoke for itself.

Sobbing now, she gave one last desperate yank.

And she was free.

"Dr. Foulke? Are you listening?" Cage's voice echoed in the room. The egg timer hit zero and dinged. The buzzing ended with a thump, and the shower cut loose with a pressurized spray of acid and base, which hissed when they touched each other, forming chloride gas.

Meg screamed and rolled out from underneath the lab bench. She scrambled to her hands and knees, her legs too cramped to run. She banged into another bench, trapped between the solid surface and the spreading pool of foaming liquid. The only escape was out into the main aisle.

Directly into Annette's line of fire.

Sobbing, gasping, praying for help though there seemed to be none to have, Meg flung herself across the lab space, headed for the door. She stopped dead when she saw the crude device wired to the door, blinking with a malevolent red light.

She'd forgotten about the booby traps.

Halfway across the room, near the windows, Annette turned. Her face creased into a smile of sick satisfaction. She raised Erik's service revolver two-handed. Aimed. Tightened her finger on the trigger.

"Get away from her!" A blur erupted through the shot-out window and launched itself at Annette.

Meg's brain jammed on the image of Erik, his face nearly gray beneath its normal healthy pallor, coming through the window. From outside. From *five stories* up.

To save her.

Time stopped. The universe collided in a logjam of relief and disbelief, fear and hot, hard longing.

Erik had come. He'd climbed. For her.

He staggered and fell, and turned the fall into a roll that saved his life when Annette fired where he'd just been. He slammed his shoulder into her legs, driving her back three steps, then regained his feet, yanked his weapon from the small of his back and turned to Meg.

Their eyes met. The contact arced between them, a complicated mix of things they'd said that morning and other things left unsaid.

Like *I love you.*

His eyes flashed with fury and he shouted, "Run, damn it!"

Annette turned and fired. A force slammed into Meg's forearm, pressure and impact without pain. Then the pain followed, along with a spurt of blood.

She stared at her wrist, at the through-and-through bullet wound beside the acid burns.

And the world sped up to a blur.

"Meg!" Erik's agonized shout battered through the shock. She turned, expecting another bullet.

Instead, Annette flung the empty gun aside and ran toward the door. To the blinking unit wired to the door.

Erik raised his gun and sighted, but Meg yelled, "No! She's got the trigger!"

She saw his expression, saw the moment of decision as Annette reached for the box, holding the remote detonator in her hand.

Erik lunged for Meg and grabbed her around the waist. "Come on. Let's get the hell out of here!"

"There's no way out!" Annette howled, her voice escalating over a weird, cackling laugh that didn't sound male or female. Hell, it barely sounded human.

When Erik dragged her toward the window, pain

tore through Meg's soul, sharper than the agony in her arm. "My lab!"

The words emerged in a fit of coughing as the chloride gas diffused throughout the room.

"Leave it. You're more important." He grabbed her arm, fingers biting deep in a pressure that seemed to convey more than he'd said. "Out."

He boosted her up onto the windowsill as Annette's laughter soared and she screamed, "If I can't have it, nobody can!"

In a blur, Meg found herself outside the building, five stories up, precariously balanced on a narrow ledge. She was facing out with her back to the wall and nothing but air in front of her to grab on to.

Then Erik was there, pressing her flat with his body, urging her away from the window. "Get to the corner. Go!"

A gigantic, rending explosion sounded in the lab. The wall shuddered and Meg screamed when her foot slipped.

"Hang on!" He banded his arm across her waist. "Turn around. There's room, and it's more like free-climbing when you're facing the wall. Bouldering. Whatever you want to call it."

Smoke and flames billowed through the window beside them. Another explosion sounded, deeper inside the lab. The stone wall heaved as though it might buckle at any moment.

Blinded by tears, choking on sobs and the burn of chloride gas, Meg did as he ordered, reversing her position so her cheek was pressed against the rapidly heating stone.

He was right. The position felt more secure. Her flats weren't climbing shoes, but she could feel the ledge with her toes.

"There's a seam above your head," his voice said in her ear, making her aware that he was pressed against her with masculine strength, his body between her and the noxious smoke coming from the lab window. His voice was tight when he said, "Reach up and use it for balance. We've got to move."

He hustled her to the corner while the building quivered and shook. Deep rumbles sounded from within, the sound growing fainter as they moved away from the window. Away from her lab. Her life's work.

"Stay with me," he said when her feet faltered. "We can't stop now. You're going to have to swing around the corner—there's an identical ledge on the other side. Trust me."

She turned her head and looked at him, really looked at him, and saw the strength of determination, the power of the man he'd once been, the man he'd found again somewhere along the line when she wasn't looking.

She nodded. "I trust you."

With the warm strength of him at her back, she wedged the fingers of her good hand into the overhead seam in the wall, took a breath, said a prayer, and pushed off to swing around the corner.

An explosion blew out the wall behind her, even as she found her toehold on the new side of the building.

"Erik!" Her heart stopped dead in her chest and she peered around the corner. *"Erik!"*

Strong fingers grabbed her good wrist and pulled her away from the corner, startling a scream out of her. She looked back to find a cop on the ledge with her, wearing riot gear and a safety rope. "This way, ma'am, and quickly. The wall could go any moment."

She yanked away from his touch, the motion almost sending her off the side of the building. For a moment she felt as though she were flying. Then that moment was gone and she was nothing more than a scared woman, years older than she'd been when she'd jumped out of perfectly good planes for fun.

But she had something now that she hadn't had back then.

A man worth living for. A man worth fighting for.

Favoring her wounded wrist, which left a gory blood trail on the reddish stonework, she worked her way back to the corner, heart pounding with fear, eyes blurred with tears at the thought that she might already be too late. She might already have lost him, with the last words between them angry ones because she'd been too stubborn, too convinced of her own cause to listen to his.

"Erik?" The word was little more than a whisper as she stuck her head around the corner and saw nothing.

The wall was gone, the ledge a smoldering wreck.

Her lungs closed on the foul air, on the knowledge that she'd lost him.

Meg. She thought she heard him whisper her name, thought for one mad, crazy moment that his ghost had so quickly come to haunt her.

Then she saw it.

The tip of a gunmetal-gray cane was hooked over the farthest corner of the ledge.

ERIK HEARD HER SHOUT his name, and he saw her head appear, seeming farther away than she should have been.

His heat-slicked fingers slipped on the smooth metal bore of the cane until he was clinging to the very end. He scrabbled for purchase with his feet, but found nothing but air and fear.

"Go!" he shouted. "Get out of here before the whole wall collapses!"

Her head disappeared, and for an instant he thought she'd listened to him. Relief battled despair. Then her face reappeared, the face he would forever hold in his heart. She shouted, "Grab this! We've got you!"

A fat black rope snaked down, knotted at the end.

Part of him feared he would pull her off the wall, but the larger part of him trusted her not to be stupid. And for the first time in a long time, in the eight years since that fateful bank robbery, he saw the future, saw himself with Meg—with his cane, without, it didn't matter anymore. His leg wasn't nearly as important as he'd let it become.

She was important. *They* were important.

Love was important.

He grabbed the rope and tangled his legs around it. Then he unhooked the cane.

And swung free as the wall beside him crumbled.

ONCE THEY'D HAULED Erik to safety, Meg lost herself in the ensuing mad scramble, a blur of flak-jacket-wearing cops, rescue personnel and researchers being evacuated from nearby labs and floors. The entire hospital was put on alert, but it seemed as though the structural damage had been contained to the Corning Lab, where the destruction had been complete.

Her lab was gone. Her work was gone. She had backup computer files stored on the hospital intranet, of course, but she would have to rebuild the rest.

Oddly, that didn't bother her nearly as much as it ought to. Maybe it was the dulling effects of shock as she was rushed down to the ER and given priority and a vascular surgery consult on her injured arm.

But more than that, she thought it was the man who stayed beside her every step of the way, the one who, once they'd pulled him in through a relatively safe window, had caught her in his arms, kissed her fiercely and whispered something she hadn't quite heard.

It wasn't until they'd installed her in an exam room and given her a hit of lidocaine that she had a moment alone with Erik.

The harsh overhead fluorescents weren't exactly

candlelight, and the smell of antiseptic was a far cry from roses and home cooking, but somehow the setting seemed just right when she took his hand in her good one and murmured, "What was that you said upstairs?"

She half expected him to brush it off, to claim that it had been the stress of the moment, of the situation. Instead he leaned down and touched his lips to hers, sending up a buzz of heat and emotion. "I said, I love you. And don't ever scare me like that again."

The words were a quick, happy punch beneath the heart. Meg felt a huge smile split her face, one that couldn't possibly reflect the enormity of the glow in her soul. "Same goes."

He grinned in return, but the shadows hadn't quite left his eyes. "Which part?"

"Both parts. I love you. And don't ever scare me like that again." Tears weren't far behind the smile. They filmed her eyes when she said, "When I saw you hanging like that…when I thought I wouldn't get back to you in time…" She faltered, not able to put it into words. Instead she slid her arm around his waist and pressed her cheek to his shirt, which smelled faintly of chloride and smoke.

The steady thump of his heart reassured her, as did the power of his arms when they closed around her. "I know." The words were as soft as the kiss he pressed to the top of her head.

Both gestures made her feel safe. Whole.

"Have you seen— Oops! Sorry, you two." Jemma

grimaced in the doorway, but her eyes held a hint of amusement. "Didn't mean to interrupt."

Erik shifted to face her, and Meg noticed that he used the cane as though it were an accessory rather than a crutch. She would have to ask him about that, and about where he'd learned to climb. But there would be time enough for that later.

"There'll be time to fool around later," he said, paralleling her thoughts exactly. "Who were you looking for?"

"I can't find Max." When Meg made a small sound of distress, Jemma immediately added, "Don't worry. He's around somewhere. But he's in a panic. Raine's gone."

Meg froze. "What do you mean, gone? She was doing so well. Was it the miscarriage? Why didn't someone—"

"No!" Jemma said quickly. "No, I'm sorry. I meant gone as in *gone.* She signed herself out against the attending's recommendation."

Erik went rigid. "What? She shouldn't. We have to get her back here whether she likes it or not." He turned to Meg. "You can do that, right? With the clotting problem?"

"Not necessarily." Meg shook her head. "She could be in real danger, or she could be fine. Factor IV Leiden is strange that way. Now that she's not pregnant…" She shrugged. "I know it's not ideal, but maybe she felt like this was the right thing to do. Maybe she needed to…get away for a while."

Erik cursed. "Get away from me, you mean."

"Or Max. Or her life." She squeezed his arm. "It's not your fault any more than it was my fault that Annette wanted what I had. She was—" Meg searched for the word "—confused. Unhappy. And she kept talking about someone named Edward. I wonder who that was. A lover maybe?"

"Her brother," a new voice said from the doorway. Detective Peters stepped inside, looking tired. "A computer search turned up her next of kin—her mother, who died last year, and her twin brother Edward, who died in his teens. Leukemia."

Meg winced. "She never spoke of it. Heck, she never talked much at all." She paused. "I can't help thinking that I should have helped her. I don't know. Somehow." She glanced at Erik. "In the lab, she talked about being a woman, how her mother told her she'd never get ahead. How things would've been better if she'd been born a man. I guess…" She swallowed and forced herself to recall those last few horrifying moments in the lab. "I guess she was trying to prove herself at Boston General. Trying to prove that her mother was right. Then I came in and started making waves with my work. With who I am. I never realized."

Erik tightened his arm around her waist, supporting her even though she knew his thoughts remained at least partly on Raine's disappearance. "Not your fault. It sounds like her mother did a number on her."

Peters nodded. "We're searching Annette's place now, and should be able to piece together more of it in the next few days. Regardless, she's gone. Her remains have been removed from the crime scene, and there's no doubting the identification. You two—" he included Meg and Erik in his gesture "—and your employees are safe. Back to business as usual."

Business as usual. The words gave Meg another wince and a kink of uncertainty as the ER doctor arrived with the vascular surgeon and shooed Erik, Jemma and the detective out of the room. She answered the doctors' questions and followed their instructions to move her fingers in sequence, then held still for another set of X-rays. But all the while, her brain churned with fuzzy thoughtlets and impossible wishes.

By the time they had her wrist sewn up and wrapped in a mile of bandages, she had her plan. Maybe midsurgery wasn't the best time to make life-altering decisions, but it was like free falling—sometimes the quickest decisions made under pressure were the best ones. Knowing it, she made the necessary phone call from her room before she gave the okay for the nurses to let Erik in.

Zachary Cage arrived on his heels, causing Erik to raise his eyebrows askance.

"I called him," Meg said. She felt a faint flutter in her stomach and told herself she was doing the right thing. "I asked him to bring the paperwork. It's time to do your deal."

Erik went still. "You're dropping your opposition to the sale?"

"You can have the NPT." She took a deep breath

and told herself that everything would be okay. "I trust you to develop the technique fairly and ethically."

When Cage handed her the paperwork, she signed beside his signature and that of a committee head, without a murmur, having read and reread every word of it over the past two weeks. The sale stripped her of all control of the NPT technology.

But that was okay. She was making room for a new chapter in her life's work. One that started with the man who crossed the room in uneven strides, took the pen from her good hand with a sizzling brush of fingertips and signed on a line farther down. He capped the pen, passed the paperwork to Cage, and took her hand.

He shook it. "Congratulations on your new lab, Dr. Corning. Or would you rather I call you 'professor'?"

Maybe it was the painkillers, maybe the stress of the past few weeks, but it took a long moment for Erik's words to penetrate, even longer for them to make any sense. When they did, Meg's heart picked up a beat. She looked from Erik to Cage and back. "Professor?"

Cage grinned. "Didn't anyone ever tell you to read thoroughly before you sign on the dotted line? That's not the original deal. It's a licensing contract. FalcoTechno gets the rights to commercialize the prenatal testing, and agrees to subsidize your lab for the next five years while you examine the feasibility and technicalities of stem cell development, with the funding renewable based on results and the agreement of both parties."

Meg stared at the pages. "Wow." The room spun as the butterflies in her stomach expanded to fly outward, fluttering through her veins in winding paths of disbelief and joy. "Wow." Then she looked up at Erik and found him watching her with all the love in the world shining in his dark eyes. "I was ready to give it to you. All of it."

He smiled. "I'm giving it back." Then he lifted an eyebrow. "Of course, you realize that I have an agenda."

She laughed and set the butterflies free. Or maybe she was the one who was finally free, because it felt an awful lot like she was flying when she said, "As long as it involves candlelight and spaghetti, I'm in."

He pulled her close, being mindful of the bandages. "It's a date. Tonight, and every tomorrow after that."

They kissed, sealing the deal in a gesture more binding than paper and ink, and Meg realized that it wasn't the same as free-falling, after all.

Because now she had someone waiting to catch her.

* * * * *

Don't miss Jessica Andersen's next
medical thriller, Under the Microscope, on sale in
January 2007
only from Harlequin Intrigue!

RUN, ALLY! Don't be fooled by him. He's evil. Don't let him touch you!

But as the forbidding figure came through the mists toward her, Ally knew she couldn't run. His features burned with dark malevolence, and his physical domination of everything around him seemed to hold her like a net.

She'd heard the tales. She knew all about the Wolverton legend and the ghost that haunted The Willows, an elegant old mansion lost by Micha Wolverton nearly a hundred years ago. According to folklore, the estate was stolen from the Wolvertons, and Micha was killed trying to reclaim it. His dying vow was to be reunited with the spirit of his beloved wife, who'd taken her life for reasons no one would speak of, except in whispers. But Ally had never put much stock in the fantasy. She didn't believe in ghosts.

Until now—

She still didn't understand what was happening.

The figure had materialized out of the mist that lay thick on the damp cemetery soil. A cool breeze and silvery moonlight had played against the ancient stone of the crypts surrounding her, until they joined the mist, causing his body to thicken and solidify right before her eyes. That was when she realized she'd seen this man before. Or thought she had, at least.

His face was familiar…so familiar, yet she couldn't put it together. Not with him looming so near. She stepped back as he approached.

"Don't be afraid," he said. His voice wasn't what she expected. It didn't sound as if it were coming from beyond the grave. It was deep and sensual. Commanding.

"Who are you?" she managed.

"You should know. You summoned me."

"No, I didn't." She had no idea what he was talking about. Two minutes ago, she'd been crouching behind a moss-covered crypt, spying on the mansion that had once been The Willows, but was now Club Casablanca. And then this—

If he was Micah, he might be angry that she was trespassing on his property. "I'll go," she said. "I won't come back. I promise."

"You're not going anywhere."

Words snagged in her throat. "Wh-why not? What do you want?"

"If I wanted something, Ally, I'd take it. This is about need."

His words resonated as he moved within inches

of her. She tried to back away, but her feet were useless. "And you need something from me?"

"Good guess." His tone burned with irony. "I need lips, soft and surrendered, a body limp with desire."

"My lips, my bod—?"

"Only yours."

"Why? Why me?" This couldn't be Micha. He didn't want any woman but Rose. He'd died trying to get back to her.

"Because you want that, too," he said.

Wanted what? A ghost of her own? She'd always found the legend impossibly romantic, but how could he have known that? How could he know anything about her? Besides, she'd sworn off inappropriate men, and what could be more inappropriate than a ghost? She shook her head again, still not willing to admit the truth. But her heart wouldn't play along. It clattered inside her chest. The mere thought of his kiss, his touch, terrified her. This wildness, it was fear, wasn't it?

When his fingertips touched her cheek, she flinched, expecting his flesh to be cold, lifeless. It was anything but that. His skin was smooth and hot, gentle, yet demanding. And while his dark brown eyes were filled with mystery and wonder, there was a sensitivity about them that threatened to disarm her if she looked too deeply.

"These lips are mine," he said, as if stating a universal fact that she was helpless to avoid. In truth, it was just that. She couldn't stop him.

And she didn't want to.

Find out how the story unfolds in...
DECADENT
by
New York Times *bestselling author*
Suzanne Forster.
On sale November 2006.

Harlequin Blaze—*Your ultimate destination*
for red-hot reads.
With six titles every month, you'll never guess
what you'll discover under the covers...

SAVE UP TO $30! SIGN UP TODAY!

INSIDE *Romance*

The complete guide to your favorite
Harlequin®, Silhouette® and Love Inspired® books.

✓ Newsletter ABSOLUTELY FREE! No purchase necessary.

✓ Valuable coupons for future purchases of Harlequin,
  Silhouette and Love Inspired books in every issue!

✓ Special excerpts & previews in each issue. Learn about all
  the hottest titles before they arrive in stores.

✓ No hassle—mailed directly to your door!

✓ Comes complete with a handy shopping checklist
  so you won't miss out on any titles.

- -

SIGN ME UP TO RECEIVE INSIDE ROMANCE
ABSOLUTELY FREE
(Please print clearly)

_____
Name

_____
Address

_____
City/Town   State/Province   Zip/Postal Code

Please mail this form to:
(098 KKM EJL9)
In the U.S.A.: Inside Romance, P.O. Box 9057, Buffalo, NY 14269-9057
In Canada: Inside Romance, P.O. Box 622, Fort Erie, ON L2A 5X3
OR visit http://www.eHarlequin.com/insideromance

IRNBPA06R   ® and ™ are trademarks owned and used by the trademark owner and/or its licensee.

SPECIAL EDITION™

Silhouette Special Edition brings you a
heartwarming new story from the *New York Times*
bestselling author of *McKettrick's Choice*

LINDA LAEL MILLER

Sierra's Homecoming

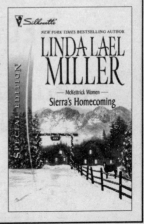

Sierra's Homecoming
follows the parallel lives
of two McKettrick women,
living their lives in the
same house but
generations apart,
each with a special son
and an unlikely new
romance.

December 2006

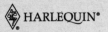
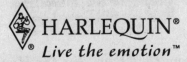

This holiday season, cozy up with

HARLEQUIN® *Romance*

 **In November
we're proud to present**

JUDY CHRISTENBERRY
Her Christmas Wedding Wish

A beautiful story of love and family found.

And

LINDA GOODNIGHT
Married Under The Mistletoe

Don't miss this installment of

The Brides of Bella Lucia

From the Heart. For the Heart.

REQUEST YOUR FREE BOOKS!

2 FREE NOVELS PLUS 2 FREE GIFTS!

HARLEQUIN®
INTRIGUE®

Breathtaking Romantic Suspense

YES! Please send me 2 FREE Harlequin Intrigue® novels and my 2 FREE gifts. After receiving them, if I don't wish to receive any more books, I can return the shipping statement marked "cancel." If I don't cancel, I will receive 6 brand-new novels every month and be billed just $4.24 per book in the U.S., or $4.99 per book in Canada, plus 25¢ shipping and handling per book and applicable taxes, if any*. That's a savings of close to 15% off the cover price! I understand that accepting the 2 free books and gifts places me under no obligation to buy anything. I can always return a shipment and cancel at any time. Even if I never buy another book from Harlequin, the two free books and gifts are mine to keep forever.

182 HDN EEZ7   382 HDN EEZK

Name	(PLEASE PRINT)

Address	Apt.

City	State/Prov.	Zip/Postal Code

Signature (if under 18, a parent or guardian must sign)

Mail to Harlequin Reader Service®:

IN U.S.A.
P.O. Box 1867
Buffalo, NY
14240-1867

IN CANADA
P.O. Box 609
Fort Erie, Ontario
L2A 5X3

Not valid to current Harlequin Intrigue subscribers.

Want to try two free books from another line?

Call 1-800-873-8635 or visit www.morefreebooks.com.

* Terms and prices subject to change without notice. NY residents add applicable sales tax. Canadian residents will be charged applicable provincial taxes and GST. This offer is limited to one order per household. All orders subject to approval. Credit or debit balances in a customer's account(s) may be offset by any other outstanding balance owed by or to the customer. Please allow 4 to 6 weeks for delivery.

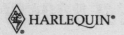